Knowing Your Identity

Knowing Your Identity

Knowing Your Identity

Doris V. McRae

Copyright © 2022 by M&M Publications. All rights reserved. No part of this publication may be reproduced, distributed, or transmitted in any form or by any means including photocopying, recording, or other electronic or mechanical methods, without the prior written permission of the publisher, except in the case of brief quotations embodied in critical reviews and certain other noncommercial uses permitted by copyright law.

M&M Publications

No part of this book may be reproduced in any form or by any means, electronic or mechanical, including photography, recording, or any information storage or retrieval system without permission in writing from the publisher.

Sale of this book without a front cover, it may have been reported stolen to the publisher. Therefore, M& M Publications is not responsible.

Compilation and Introduction copyright © 2022 by M & M Publications.

Library of Congress Card Number

ISBN: TBA

Knowing Your Identity credits:

Author: Doris V. McRae

Typist: Carolyn Getter-McRae

Knowing Your Identity

Publicist: Country McRae

Promoter: Country McRae

Cover Concepts: Mya

Published by M&M Publications

E-Mail: mmcrae749@gmail.com

Printed in the U.S.A.

Knowing Your Identity

Doris V. McRae

From the Heart

Now... for my deepest show of gratitude, I want to thank God for my immeasurable talent. When it comes to pen and paper, God you've blessed me with the strokes of Michelangelo. It's because of you Lord that I'm able to tell a story and also paint the picture, in my audience mind. Again... God...I'm nothing without you. I want to thank my grandson, Country and his wife, Carolyn Getter-McRae for taking the time to come out of their comfort zone and publish my book. Trust...it's a must that we lift up the name of Jesus. I'm really lost for words; because...this has always been my dream, to be on such a very big platform, to tell all about the blessings of the Lord. He's brought me through a many of storms. I can't help to praise his name. I want to send my love to my husband, Mr. Colon McRae Sr. Together we've been blessed with six beautiful kids. John Allen McRae (R.I.P.), Annie Lee McRae, Peggy Dixon, Colon McRae Jr.(R.I.P), Sandra D. McRae, and Ronald A. McRae(R.I.P.). I'm so blessed to have raised you all. It wasn't me. God did it !!!

Also...I'm blessed to be apart of all of my grand and great grandchildren's lives !!! To my family Rufus, John, and James Bullock. God has really blessed me to have strong brothers as you all. Also....a special shout out to my cousin, Mrs. Arnetta Lee. You're a cousin that I know was sent from the heavens. And...I love you so very much!!! To my nieces and nephews Mary Saunders, Dianne, Edna and Emma, Billy (R.I.P.), Joseph (R.I.P), James, Rodney, and Tony Bullock ; know that your aunt loves you above and beyond measure...

A special show of love to the McRae, Bullock, Peguese, Bostic, Daye, and Chamber's family. Know that you all hold a very special place in my heart.

Knowing Your Identity

A big show of love to, Pastor Linda Perry of First Congregation United Church of Christ. Thaaaaaanks for being our shepherd and keeping us in the pastures of God. You're so very special and I want to say that I love you so very much !!!

Knowing Your Identity

From The Heart

This is such a very special project to us. Know matter what, we do know that, we are nothing without God... Publishing this book, and putting it out on the market, for God is a must. It's so very important that everyone knows their identity when it comes to being children of God. M&M Publications don't only publish Urban fiction. We do what is right, when it comes to opening a persons eyes to know that with God we can make it. Again...it was an honor to publish and promote my grandmother's book.

Country & Carolyn Getter-McRae

This book is dedicated to my Grandmother, mother and brother

Mrs. Emma Swann, Mrs. Olivia (Hatch) Swann, and James Edward Jr.

I love and miss you all. R.I.P

Knowing Your Identity

Doris V. McRae

Knowing Your Identity

Introduction

Speaking positive things in life through rough times is true power... It's not just about having faith as the size of a mustard seed. The main scenario of being able, to move mountain's by the word, is knowing your true identity, as far as being a child of God. A lot of people today go to church faithfully. Even though they show up, go to the alter for prayer, tithe, receive a soothing soul from the choirs song, and hear a powerful sermon from the preacher; Still...when they leave, as far as being a saved child of God, somehow they forget their identity. I do know and understand; because...I've been there and done that. I know how Satan whispers in our ear. That whisper today, I've learned to recognize. Being able to also see the devils plan and schemes, comes from the true powerful spiritual essence of Almighty God. Those powers that I've learned from God are not to keep to myself. It's my duty to share the message of spiritual freedom. It's time that all children of God take heed. Even though we say that we are deep, and rooted in Christ, I want to know, do you know the powers that we possess. If you don't, together we can make it happen. Under the blood of Jesus, let's tap into the source!!! This book will give power, insight, and also ammunition, to cast Satan out of your way...

Being children of God we are marked. It's because we are royal heirs to the throne of God!!! This book tells us all about our identity. If you are one whose lost your way, due to a certain detour in life, which has caused you to get defocused of your identity, I ask you to give me just a little bit of your time.

Jesus died on the cross for our sins and transgressions at Calvary. God sacrificed his only begotten son for each and every last one of us. That way each of us will be accountable for our own salvation. We've heard the word from preachers, our parents, on the radio, on television, in neighborhoods, and shopping centers. There is no excuse when it comes to our one on one with God. If you do not know where you stand with God, today, is the day, from this point on, you'll know. Enjoy this special word. It was meant for you!!!

Knowing Your Identity

Chapter 1

Speaking

Genesis Chapter 1

Verses 1-31

This chapter shows the power of God. By mouth God spoke the world into existence. If you look at the scriptures mostly all of them begin with "God said." We are walking on an earth, and living in a universe, which was spoken up by God. Those same powers we possess. How was God able to speak the world into existence? Have you ever asked yourself that? I'm going to tell you how. It's because God knew that he was God. My question is, do you know who you are because, God resides inside of you. We are heirs to God's Kingdom. Just like God we have the power to move burdens by speaking to them. We have the power to speak healing to the sick. We have the power to speak life over death. We have the power to speak sight to the blind, and we have the power to speak to the poor and make them rich. It's called speaking and planting the seed of victory. That seed of victory that we plant is going to sprout and grow inside of people or circumstances faster than ever. In order for that to happen though, we got to know our identity. For instance the job economy is tough right now. That's just a worldly issue though. Spiritual, especially when you are a child of God, always conquer worldly issues. I say this because, the devil will whisper in your ear that, "You can't get that job" or "Those people aren't going to hire you." He'll even tell you "Don't waste your gas job hunting the economy is too bad."

Knowing Your Identity

Being a child of God that's when your ego should kick in and say, "Satan in the name of Jesus, evidently you don't know who I am. I'm on a mission to get a job, and that mission, I will achieve."

Just right then and there, you spoke your job into existence, and you spoke it with faith, due to knowing your identity. Speaking like that as far as job issues, you might as well go on ahead and get ready to clock in on somebody's payroll, or get ready for set salary. Being a child of God, and knowing your identity, you can have it any way you want it. God can do the impossible. Another example for instance: In life when it comes to our kids, sometimes things we say can be harmful, or helpful to them. What I'm about to share happens in a lot of households not only in our country but all over the world.

Things we say can register inside of our kids. Remember we have the ability to speak things into existence. If you say to your child; "You can't do that," as far as conquering a dream. Or you say "That won't work out." That's just what's going to happen. Nothing will work out because we planted a seed of discouragement. That seed will sprout and will blossom. Our kids will begin to have dwarfed goals and colorless dreams.

They will began to live up to the expectations of nothing will work out for them. It's because it was spoken upon them. Now on the other hand, speaking positive things into your child's life is pure power. "You can accomplish anything that you set out to do, when it comes to goals and dreams." Even when it comes down to school, "You are so very smart and you will pass your grades with flying colors." That seed that you plant will make or break your child's destiny. Even if your son or daughter has experienced some difficult times even

Knowing Your Identity

though you've spoke positive things in their lives, because as children of God we are always subject for attack by the devil, still speak positive things into their lives. The word of God, outweighs worldly issues, and it will always bring forth prosperity. If they are on drugs, they'll eventually get clean. If they go to jail or prison, they'll get tired, and will have a brand new life. Their whole life will be in line with God's destiny for them. We must keeping speaking the word over their lives for the better.

Even when we get sick we can't say, "I'm sick." We must say I'm doing just fine. Then that's just what's going too happened. We are going to get better. No matter how we feel, all we have to do is speak it, and healing will begin to take place. Now this is a topic that really needs to be discussed. It has to do with financial situations. I've heard people say that they were poor as far as figure of speech. Remember what we say comes into existence.

Children of God should never claim being poor. We should always say that we are rich because we are. We are plugged into a powerful source which is God. Our father is rich. Remember, this with all of your heart. Not only speak that you are rich, know that you are a royal heir to the kingdom. We are rich in spirit and power. All we have to do is know our identity.

Even when it comes to saying this is going to be a bad day. If we say that our day is going to be bad, that's just what it's going to be. Things won't seem to go right at work and you'll find your job quite a task that's hectic. Even when it comes to working with your associates, you'll find yourself not so sociable and you'll distance yourself. It's because of how you outlined your day due to what you said.

Knowing Your Identity

Now, if you wake up in the morning, and thank God for a beautiful day; that's just what you're going have. A beautiful day. On the way to work, traffic will go just fine. Once you get to work you'll see it as a beautiful atmosphere. Your job task goes smooth, and you'll find yourself able to socialize with other associates in the work place. It's all because you spoke a beautiful day into existence. No matter if the day is dreary or even raining, if you say that it's going to be a beautiful day. That's just what your day is going to be. No matter what, it will be as a nice sunny day. That's why we got to understand our identity. God gave us as his children, the power to speak things into existence. Remember speak good things and watch how they come into existence. God gave us that power. It tells us all about it in. Genesis Chapter 1 verses 1-31. This covers the topic of speaking.

Knowing Your Identity

Chapter 2

Marked

Genesis Chapter 3 verses 1-22

While we are on this powerful topic of knowing your identity, did you know by us being a child of God's, we are considered marked. Adam and Eve were in the Garden of Eden. In the garden the serpent, which was the devil, manipulated Eve to eat the fruit from the tree of the knowledge of good and evil, which God forbade them not to do. Being deceived, not only did Eve eat of the fruit, she also shared it with her husband, Adam. Due to the devil's tricks, this was a test. Adam and Eve committed the first sin, disobedience. On this spiritual walk that we are on, fruit which God has told us not to eat will be presented to us each and every day. Remember...We are marked and the devil is going to come at us anyway that he can. Notice he showed up as a serpent. We are dealing with a wicked spiritual power that's out to steal our joy. The devil is out to kill you and destroy your identity.

The thing about it is, when this fruit is presented to us we have to not only recognize it, but, we must know and look at who's presenting it to us. Here are a few examples that may give you better insight, so you will be able to see more clearly. The blessings that God puts in our lives, which causes us to shine like pure gold, the devil will do whatever it takes to cause our gold to tarnish. I'm speaking of our walk. In the church a lot of us come from different walks of life. Some of us have overcome depression from issues of life. Also others may have suffered from unhealthy relationships; other issues could even be sickness, drugs,

Knowing Your Identity

alcoholism, and gambling. For instance, you may have suffered from drug addiction, and God has redeemed you, a complete turnaround. Then one day you are at the neighborhood convenience store.

Now...when you pulled up in the parking space in front of the store, you got out and went inside, got your merchandise, paid for it, and walked out of the store. As you were walking to your car, you noticed something on the ground, and it turns out to be your former drug of choice, that was suddenly dropped or appeared from out of nowhere.

Now...you haven't indulged in 10 years, and all of a sudden, you're caught alone just like Eve was. There goes the devil again presenting fruit that is no good for you. Even when it comes to unhealthy relationships, when you know that someone is bad for you due to past issues. It took you sometime to get over that person. All of a sudden, you're in a new relationship, with the one God sent.

When that person sees you doing well with your new soulmate, fiancé', or wife, From out of nowhere, here they come. Once they see a chance to slip their phone number to you, for you to call them, do you do it? That's the devil. Because...he wants to destroy all that God blesses you with. Gambling is also a bad habit. If you have a nice home, family, and cars, the devil will come to you as one of your former gambling buddies. He will invite you over to his house for a friendly game of poker, which will turn into gambling for money. Next thing you know you're back on the road to gambling again. It's so very important that we recognize the enemy and the fruits that he bare. If you have been redeemed from alcohol, God bless you because alcoholism is tough to overcome.

Knowing Your Identity

Always be on guard because the devil knows this. You'll find yourself at work and a co-worker will say "After work how about a drink?" It's who's in your friend. The same way the devil use the serpent, he uses people. It has to do with our identity. I've never been a part of these circumstances but I've heard many testimonies. What has taken place is God knew us from our mother's womb. Due to that a seed of dominion was planted inside of us to reign and be blessed. The devil knows this that's why we are considered marked. It's the devil duty to stop us from prospering. That's why all of a sudden bad issues come our way. Knowing our identity, we know that we are highly protected.

It's not about what we go through, it's how we come out of it. All we have to do, is ask God for the spiritual essence to recognize, when the enemy is presenting these fruits to us. If it's something that will cause us to be disobedient to our loved ones, it's bad for us. If it's something to cause us to go to jail, it's bad for us. If it's something that will not make our parents proud, we don't need to be involved in it. The devils' job is to strip us of the kingdom of heaven. Our identity is so very powerful and things that are not of God we attract.

Due to this topic I challenge you to pay close attention because the devil is going to come at us in full force. The main scenario about this whole ordeal is, God has given us the spiritual powers, to see these fruits that the devil presents to us day after day. Remember….pay close attention, because, by us being children of God the devil is going to come because we are marked by God's glory.

Knowing Your Identity

Chapter 3

Give Your Best

Genesis Chapter 4

Verses 1-5

As far as our identity as being children of God, we are so very blessed. Even though we experience a few storms we always come out of the rain. Coming out of the storms is not by our power. We come out because of the power of God. In any shape, form, or fashion; God always gives us his best. Some of us have no alarm clocks to wake us up. Somehow we get up in the morning on time for work. Matter of fact, let me back up a little further than that. Who wakes us up in the morning? It's God who wakes us up. So it's a true fact. God does give us his best because, today wasn't promised.

I want to go over these scriptures with you in Genesis Chapter 4 verses 1-5. It's about two brothers Cain and Abel. It refers to the gifts that they presented to the Lord.

As we know God blessed both Cain and Abel with agriculture talents. Cain was born with a prosperous green thumb. He tilled the land, dropped seeds, and enormous crops produced. Cain had the prettiest corn, string beans, cabbage, cucumbers, watermelon, etc. These crops also stretched for miles and miles. Each season crops always had a major harvest.

Knowing Your Identity

Now his brother Abel, as I also shared, dealt in agriculture as well. He dealt with livestock. He tended to goats, cattle, chickens, turkeys, pigs, and sheep. Abel's livestock was healthy because they were very well provided for by him. There was plenty meat and vegetables around the household. God allowed them to eat the fat of the land by his many blessings, which were their talents.

Now it was God who wanted to see how thankful Cain and Abel were for all of the blessings that were bestowed upon them.

In verse 3, this is how Cain showed god his appreciation.

Listen to this scripture:

And in the process of time it came to pass that Cain brought an offering of the fruit of the ground to the Lord.

Now listen to what Abel done in verse 4:

Abel also brought of the first born of his flock and of their fat. And the Lord respected Abel and his offering.

Do you see the difference in those two scriptures? Cain was blessed with a prosperous green thumb. Whatever ground that he tilled, seed that he planted, brought forth major crops. I'm sure that Cain watered his crops but God made it rain. God has blessed Cain far and beyond measure. But... look at how Cain showed God how much that he was thankful.

First of all in the process of time, it came to pass that Cain brought an offering of the fruit of the ground to the Lord. The word process means: In the course of

Knowing Your Identity

time. Basically, this means that there was procrastination as far as Cain bringing his offerings to God because he had to process his thoughts. Cain was greedy and he wanted it all. Instead of him giving God his best, he gave God the slackest of the slack. He gave God as far as offering half ripe watermelons, scorched corn, half ripe strawberries, and shriveled up string beans. Cain showed God just how much he appreciated the talents that he blessed him with. As you can also see in the scripture that God didn't respect Cain's offering and his countenance fell.

Now if you are lost when it comes to the definition of countenance it means: To express approval.

God's golden of approval of Cain tarnished. It's because Cain held back when it was time to give God his best.

Now Abel that keeper of the livestock this was pleasing to God's sight when he brought his offerings before God. As it says in the scripture in verse 4: Abel brought of the firstborn of his flock and of their fat.

The firstborn is special, and I'm sure that as far as the first of Abel's flock, it was hard to give away. Now when it comes to the word fat, it has nothing to do with weight. Fat has two definitions. This particular fat defines: To have the best of everything.

All of Abel's flock was top notch. Still he didn't hold back when it was time to give his offering in livestock to the Lord. Abel's countenance didn't fall either. It soared in God's sight higher than ever. In life no matter how hard it get, we got to do, and give our best. Then... God will do the rest. When God blesses us with talents that benefits us. We've got to show him our appreciation.

Knowing Your Identity

Just like you may have been riding the bus for a while. It's because the money that we made on our jobs caused us to be on a strict budget. After paying rent, utilities, gas, and grocery bills, we have no money for car notes. Then suddenly we land a new job or got a raise on our current job which allows us to be able to afford a car. Make sure that we take the time to see how it all took place for us to get a new car. We've got to thank God. I say this is because he knows and feels all of our cares and concerns. The car he knew that you needed it. It may not have come when you wanted it but, it came right on time. Continue to give God your best. Go to church, praise him, and share the glory of God with others, as far as how he's worked in your life.

Show God how much you thank him by your tithes. Even when you are laying or sitting around and you may all of sudden hear "Get on your knees and pray to me," as if you are watching your favorite television show. It may sound crazy but, at that moment, put the television show to the side, and get on your knees and praise God.

What do you do when you are in church and the preacher is putting out a powerful sermon? The spirit is all over you. The thing about it is, you want to let God have his way with you because, of what people will think. Don't hold back. Let God have his way because, that could be the major moment for a break through. God Loves when we show up and show out for him. It's such a pleasing sight in his eyes. Giving our best to God is not hard to do because he gives us his best each and every day. It shouldn't be something that we have to debate or think about. We should never hold back anything from God. Don't be like Cain and be slack towards God. Be like Abel and give God the fat of the land. Again… give God your best, and he'll do the rest. It's a part of our identity.

Knowing Your Identity

Chapter 4

Let it go

Exodus Chapter 2

Verses 2-10

This passage is about Moses and all that he's went through at birth. After the reign and death of Joseph, a new pharaoh took over. The Hebrew people were no longer looked on as individuals that Joseph established them to be. They became slaves. Manual labor such as working in the field, landscaping, cleaning around the palace, and making bricks for construction, was done around the clock. As the Egyptians worked the Hebrew people over the years, the Hebrew population began to multiply even though they were slaves.

Pharaoh the king, seen it with his own eyes, because, the Hebrew women were giving birth to children on a regular basis as 9-11 months apart. What really caught Pharaoh's attention is that mostly the Hebrew women were having boys. That also represented strength in the days to come. For the Hebrew people Pharaoh worried about being able to not control them for labor purposes and also the rise of war.

The king sent out a demanding warrant by mouth to kill all of the boys that the Hebrew women gave birth to. Moses was his mother's first son. She refused to let anything happened to him. Even though Pharaoh the king himself issued this warrant for her son, Moses' mother still refused to go along with the

Knowing Your Identity

program. She hid him for three months. Then a major decision had to be made. Let's look at verse 3 and see what she did.

Verse 3: But when she could no longer hide him, she got a papyrus basket for him, double it with asphalt and pitch, put the child in it, and laid it in the reeds by the river's bank.

This may sound ridiculous but, Moses' mother walked her son to the river, laid him down, and put him in it.

I'm sure as she held the basket that he laid in, the decision to let him go down the river, was very tough, and drastic.

Still being a woman of God, with strong faith, she bent down with the basket, as Moses laid in it, and let it go. Baby Moses floated on down the river. Pharaoh's daughter was bathing in the river and she noticed the basket. Once she saw it she told one of the maid servants who accompanied her to go and get it. From that very day, God used Moses, as a purpose for his glory. It all begun from a drastic decision on his mother's behalf on whether to hold on to him or let him go.

That happens today in life when we have to let things go. I'm not talking about putting our babies in a basket and letting them float down Eno River. What I'm talking about is making strong positive decisions by faith. Just like Moses' mother, when we are faced with tough life issues, that only God can solve, we need to let go and let God handle it. A lot of solutions that I've faced in the past. I used to make terrible decisions as far as finding a solution to the

Knowing Your Identity

problem. Knowing who I am as far as my identity, I've realized over time that I need to seek God, and make decisions on the count of my faith in him.

It's that time again. Let's discuss a few examples that apply to what goes on in our lives everyday as far as the things that we need to let go.

On your job you may be a very good employee. You are always on time. The social skill that you possess causes everyone at work to look forward to you being there. As far as your job skills, your performance is so very outstanding. Basically, I'm saying that you contribute to a nice work atmosphere.

Here's the problem though, even though you are a very good employee, your boss always seems to come down on you. He or she, always seem to brush off things that you say, when you're trying to discuss work related issue with them, Even in the mornings or evenings that you come in, and speak to your boss, he or she may give you a crabby look. Your boss may even say "What's so good about this morning or evening." Due to feeling insulted you'd probably want to give your boss a little piece of your mind. Being a child of God we must do what may seem crazy to the flesh but, spiritually we need to let it go, when it comes to our attitude. Look at the big picture. Telling the boss off could cause a very hostile work environment. It also could cause you to lose your job. With the economy like it is jobs are so very hard to come by.

A job is something that we can't afford to lose. When we ignore these types of issues, it doesn't make us spiritual weaklings. We become spiritually strong. Also letting issues such as these go, brings the true blessings of God. Being able

Knowing Your Identity

to look over issues that may cause the flesh to want to react in a bad way, it's in our identity as children of God to over work them.

When Moses' mother let him go, he became a powerful vessel for God. He led the children of Israel out of the strong bondage of Egypt, across the Red Sea, which was parted by Moses raising up his hands unto God, to do so. That's also where our power comes from. Ask God to give you the ability, when issues rise up against you, due to negligence on someone's behalf, to let it go.

Knowing Your Identity

Chapter 5

Doing Gods Will

1st Samuel Chapter 15

Verses 1-11

God gave King Saul a mission. It was a mission to take out King Agag and all of the Amalekites. The reason was because the Amalekites continued to ambush Israel which was God's children. The most anointed. In our body, which is supposed to be the temple of God, we can't continue to flirt with sin.

Instead of Saul wiping out King Agag and the Amalekites totally like God told him too; He chose to do something that satisfied his own self gain.

Let's take a look at verse 8 and see how Saul was disobedient to God's orders.

Verse 8: He also took King Agag of the Amalekites alive, and utterly destroyed all of the people with the edge of the sword.

Again... Saul was very disobedient towards God and this is how God reacted to such behavior.

This is what God was very disobedient towards God and this is how God reacted to such behavior.

Knowing Your Identity

This is what God said in verse 11: "I greatly regret that I have set up Saul as King. For he has turned back from following me, and has not performed my commandments."

What caused God to feel this way is because of Saul's behavior. Instead of Saul following God's commandments, he chose to keep what was valuable in his eyes, wipe out everything else, an allow King Agag to live. In God's Kingdom when it comes to following his commandments we can't half step. We are to never flirt with the enemy.

God gave Saul the order because, he knew how much King Agag, and his Amalekite army, looked forward in their hearts with true hatred, to ambush Israel. Due to Israel being God's people it was time to draw the line against the Amalekites and Saul was the anointed chosen King to do just that. The whole ordeal is, he didn't live up to his identity, and handle business like God told him to. The enemy is just who he is, our enemy, and we can't flirt with our enemies because it's dangerous. In Christianity our enemy is Satan, and if we continue to flirt with him, eventually he'll wipe us out.

In this day and time as children of God we are always on the platform for ambush. Due to Satan's evil schemes and tricks, we have to always be on the lookout. Because of King Saul's disobedience, King Agag is alive still. Now he can re-establish his kingdom and ambush Israel again.

How this regards to us is, if God had given us a commandment to stay away from things or situations that is not of him or his word, we must take heed

Knowing Your Identity

because the enemy Satan will eventually ambush us in so many ways that could, and would, set us back.

His ambushes can hurt us financially, physically, and mentally. We could even lose our life due to flirting with the enemy. Us as children of God we must take heed of this message. God's commandment is our blue print to life. With his blueprint we can't lose. Flirting with the enemy also means that we are straddling the fence. We are either going to be for God or we are going to be for the devil. Being a Christian is not hard to tell when you're straddling the fence because our conscious tells us, and immediately we feel guilty. Due to selfish desires we'll go against God's commandments and do what we feel is best. It's all a part of being in the flesh.

Because Saul did what he chose to do, and went against God, he was stripped of the kingdom. From that day forth, nothing came without a struggle. That was because God allowed him to be where he wanted to be and that was with the enemy. It wasn't King Agag who was ambushing the children of Israel, it was the spirit who was in him and his army. The devil.

The spiritual theory in the scripture is; don't flirt with the devil. We can't go to church and still take part in worldly things that is not of God. The church today is so full of people who have been redeemed from different phases of life. A lot of people in the church today is a living testimony because, due to all that the devil took them through, they're not supposed to be living. It was all due to God's glory. The enemy knows this, and it's our duty as far as our identity, to know that the ambush is still on. The devil will bring anything to you that are all a

Knowing Your Identity

part of your desires. In order to be ambushed we have to be caught-off guard. Let's take a look at the definition of the word ambush.

Ambush – a surprise attack from hiding; those hiding in wait; a deception or trap – vs. To lie in wait for; to attack from hiding.

That's what the devil does to us. He's always on the prowl. We have a commandment from God that says stay away from those things that will strip us of the kingdom of God. When Saul went on and done what he chose to do, in a matter of time, he lost his kingship, and a new king was anointed by the name of King David.

He wasn't afraid to carry out God's orders when it came to war with the enemy. By us being God's anointed children, neither should we. With the word of God, stay focused by, doing his will, and go to war, when the devil tries to ambush you.

By the glory of God, you'll come out victorious, and you'll still possess your royal identity in God's eyes.

Knowing Your Identity

Chapter 6

Where do you stand?

1st Kings – Chapter 18 Verses 21-39

VERSES 21: And Elijah came to all the people and said "how long will you falter between the two options? If the Lord is God, follow him; but if Baal, follow him. "But the people answered him not a word.

VERSES 22: Then Elijah said to the people, "I alone am left a prophet of the Lord; but Baal's prophets are four hundred and fifty men.

Those two scriptures display true heart as far as Elijah's character. As you can see he stood up against four hundred and fifty men, when it came to standing up for God. Nothing or nobody could cause his mind to take a detour route because his heart was set on God. We all know that your mind can be easily changed, when it comes to how you feel about something or someone with your heart, your feelings about it or them is real. Here Elijah was on Mount Carmel standing up for God. These people who he stood up against believed in another God called Baal. We all know that there is but only one true divine God. I'm just going to put it to you plain and simple. If you follow any God besides the true God you're setting yourself up for destruction. Look at Exodus chapter 20. This is how God feels about us serving other Gods. Here's a cross reference.

Verse 3: You shall have no other Gods before me.

Knowing Your Identity

Verse 4: You shall not make for yourself a carved image-any likeness of anything that is in heaven above or in the earth beneath, or that is in the water underneath the earth.

Verse 5: You shall not bow down to them or serve them. For I, the Lord your God, am a jealous God, visiting the fathers upon the children to the third and fourth generations of those who hate me, but showing mercy to thousands, to those who love me and keep my commandments.

On this particular day on Mount Carmel not only were both parties expressing their options, but Elijah having total faith that God was king of kings, and the Lord of Lords called them out. He wanted to show them that his God would show up and also show out, whenever he called on him.

Let's look at verse 23: This is how Elijah chose to get his point across.

Verse 23: Therefore let them give us two bulls, and let them choose one bull for themselves, cut it in pieces, and lay it on the wood, but put no fire under it; and I will prepare the other bull, and lay it on the wood, but put no fire under it. How... let's also look at verse 24. This will show where Elijah stands as far as his faith in God.

Verse 24: "Then you call on the name of your gods, and I will call on the name of the Lord; and the God who answers by fire, He is God," So all the people answered and said "It is well spoken, from that point on as agreement took place.

Being who we are it is of our biggest importance to know that God is who he is, and we must stand up for him. We have to always have faith in God

Knowing Your Identity

just like Elijah did. He loved God, and he went all out to get his point across, that our God is a powerful and awesome God. We can always depend on him no matter what. Elijah knew this and that's why he stood up for God all by himself against four hundred and fifty men.

Verse 25: Now Elijah said to the prophets of Baal, "choose one bull for yourselves and prepare it first, for you are many and call on the name of your god, but put no fire under it, "Now notice in the scriptures when it refers to our awesome and powerful God, they use the capital "G," I'm here to tell you that any god compared to our God, strength and song is small.

As the scriptures goes on these prophets of Baal has set themselves up for a letdown. The prophets called on Baal. He didn't show up, they cried out to him, still no show. The prophets even went to the extreme of cutting themselves. Baal didn't come to their rescue. Elijah looked at them in total disgust because of their misconception of which God will and will always be. To show the prophets how powerful God is. Elijah told them to cut out their racket and come near.

He had to show them a thing or two. Instead of him just calling on God to send fire on the altar; he poured water on the bulls and all over the altar. Elijah wanted to show these Baal followers that God will not only light up the bulls but, he'll also light up the water too. They said water don't burn. Let me tell you our God can do anything. There is nothing that is too impossible of our God.

Knowing Your Identity

Chapter 7

The Battle is not yours

2nd Chronicles Chapter 20

Verse 1-22

Ammon, Moab, and Mt. Seir, these tribes sent threats of war towards the people of God in Judah and Jerusalem. Each one of these tribes had an enormous amount of soldiers. The Ammonites had nearly19,657. in the army of the Moabites they had 17,124. Mt. Seir, this army had only 15,523 soldiers in their army.

55,544 verses 15,523 people; Ammon, Moab, and Mt. Seir really outnumbered the people of Judah and Jerusalem. As the rumor of war surfaced throughout the region, all over Judah and Jerusalem, people walked around awestricken, and some of them were seeking ways to leave the city.

Not only were Ammon, Moab, and Mt Seir strong as far as the size of their armies. They also had high tech artillery at that day and time. They had double edge swords. Their spears were high tech. They had finger grips on them. Their armor was top of the line from head to toe. These armies even had stone launchers, combined they were a deadly force.

Can you imagine being in an army with only 13,253 soldiers. How would you feel knowing that Ammon, Moab, and Mt Seir, which was a great multitude of people rising up against you? How about even if you were the king or Queen

Knowing Your Identity

over Judah and Jerusalem. You know that when you are the King and Queen that means that you are the overseer. By you being the overseer the people of the city, state, or country are going to bring their cares and concerns to you.

In this particular case King Jehoshaphat was the king and ruler of Judah and Jerusalem. The cares and great concerns of war towards them, were brought to him each and every day, all around the clock by people in the cities and the kingdom. People were coming to the kingdom morning, noon, and night saying, "King Jehoshaphat it's 55,544 soldiers rising up to go to war against us." Then they would say, "They got launchers, spears with finger grips on them, and double edged swords. Even...their armor can't be penetrated. What are we going to do with this vast army, king?"

All of the peoples care and concerns began to weigh down on the king. Being of the flesh, he began to panic and fear. That's what the flesh causes us to do, but, there is no need though. Reason being, even though Ammon, Moab, and Mt.Seir, had such vast armies; still...they were no match at all for Judah and Jerusalem. Armor, stone launchers, doubled edged swords; that Ammon, Moab, and Mt.Seir had; still...the people of Judah and Jerusalem had the Almighty Power of God. There was no need to fear.

In verse 15. Listen to what God says to the inhabitants of Judah and Jerusalem. "Listen all you of Judah, and you inhabitants of Jerusalem, and you King Jehoshaphat! Thus says the Lord to you; Do not be afraid or dismayed because of this great multitude, for the battle is not yours, but God's."

Knowing Your Identity

Now... Let's look at verse: 17. This is so powerful what God told them.Verse:17. "You will not need to fight in this battle. Position yourselves, standstill, and watch the salvation of the lord who is with you, O Judah and Jerusalem! Do not fear or be dismayed: tomorrow go out against them, for the Lord is with you."

You must go on and read verses1-22. It's pure power and gives us total self-assurance, that no matter what kind of life issues that try to rise up against us, God will always be there to fight our battles. Notice the exclamation points at the end of the scriptures.

The definition of exclamation point is –excitement!!!! I mean this to the highest degree.

God is always excited to fight our battles. All we have to do is position ourselves, standstill and watch the salvation of the Lord take its toll on the enemy. When storms such as these arise, due to the flesh, we begin to panic and fear, just like the people of Judah and Jerusalem, and King Jehoshaphat. Just that quickly they forgot their identity.

I'm here to tell you as a living testimony. I don't care who rises up against you, or, what a situation may look or feel like. The battle is not yours. We war against bills, job issues, family situations, due to Satan's ways of craftiness. Give your cares and concerns to God. Only his power can defeat Satan who's our enemy. God is our joy and strength. Always...we will have the victory. All we have to do is position ourselves and watch the salvation of the Lord take over. Let's also look at verse 22. This will back up all that I have shared.

Knowing Your Identity

Verse 22: Now... when they began to sing and praise, the Lord set up ambushes against the people of Ammon, Moab, and Mt.Seir, which had come against Judah and Jerusalem, and they were defeated. Just like God wiped their problems out, so will wipe out ours. As far as identity as of who we are. We must always realize the battle is not ours. Its God's...

Chapter 8

Rebuilding

Ezra – Chapter 4 Verses 1-5

I love to see people who fell due to shortcomings in life, get back up from a tremendous blow from the enemy. There are people of God who fell, and because of feeling ashamed they walked away from the church. They've had difficult times with drugs, alcohol, gambling, sickness, unhealthy relationships, etc. The list goes on and on. As I've shared with you in previous chapters and heard testimonies over the year's tears fell from their eyes.

It's such a beautiful sight to see people of God get bac up and dust themselves off after they have fallen. It's because as far as their identity they recognize who they are. People of God may fall at times, but always get back up. Do you remember the Timex watch commercial? Listen to this, "It takes a lickin' but keeps on tickin'." So do we as the people of God. The main ordeal about this whole situation of getting back up is, REBUILDING.

As we have seen so far in this book.

Now let's take a look at Ezra Chapter 4 verse 1-5. This also has to do with rebuilding. On our way to rebuilding the enemy may throw a few distractions our way. Verse 1: Now when the adversaries of Judah and Benjamin heard that the descendants of the captivity were building the temple of the Lord God of Israel.

Knowing Your Identity

Verse 2: They came to Zerubbabel and the heads of the fathers' house, and said to the "Let us build with you, for we seek your God as you do: and we have sacrificed to him since the days of Esarhaddon king Assyria, who brought us here."

We always have to be on our guard at all times. The devil is cunning and as you are trying to rebuild it seems like it's so difficult and nothing is working out. But don't give up or quit. That feeling only comes from satan our adversary.

Verse 3: Bit Zerubbabel and Jeshua and the rest of the heads of the fathers' house of Israel said to them. "You may do nothing with us to build a house for our God; but we alone will build to the Lord God of Israel, as king Cyrus the king of Persia has commanded us."

Verse 4: Then the people of the land tried to discourage the people of Judah. They troubled them in building.

Verse 5: and hired counselors against them to frustrate their purpose all the days of Cyrus king of Persia, even until the reign of Darius king of Persia

In the lives of God's people who fell down has gotten back up. When it comes to rebuilding your home, family, job, finances, relationship situations; You can best believe a distraction is on the way.

Notice in the scripture verse 1, it says the adversaries of Judah and Benjamin. How can you allow an adversary to help you rebuild? The adversaries were their enemies. They weren't there to help them rebuild but as wolves in sheep clothing, ready to see their weakness in able to tear down the temple of God.

Knowing Your Identity

After those testimonies are shared with other in the church, mall, grocery stores, or even with a person who needs inspiration. Our adversary, the devil don't like that as we rebuild our temple Satan is plotting how he can tear it down. So he comes at us full force to kill steal and destroy.

Just like Zerubbabel and Jeshua on the road to building this mighty temple. When their adversaries came trying to so call help them. And they said boldly "You may do nothing with us to build a house for our God; but we alone will build to the Lord God of Israel, as King Cyrus the king of Persia has commanded us."

We've got to bold just like that towards the devil as we're rebuilding. If you allow adversaries to help you rebuild your temple will never stand. Being a child of God you may have bounced back from a difficult time being you hooked up with wrong people. As you are trying to rebuild yourself back up those so called friends will act as if they're glad for you, but still try to persuade you that is alright to be of the world every now and then.

Don't think you can do the same things and get different results. Stay focus on rebuilding your temple meaning you. Remember if you allow the adversary to help you rebuild your temple it will never stand.

Knowing Your Identity

Chapter 9

It's Just a Test

Job-Chapter 1 & 2

This is one of my favorite books in the bible. In this book we learn about Job, a very rich and powerful man who feared and also loved God. Job never went a day without thanking God for all that he's done for him. When it came to praising God there was no shame in Job at all. I mention job being a reach and powerful man. Let me give you a run down as far as how Gods' blessings rained down up him.

Job had a beautiful family, a wife, seven sons, and three daughters. He possessed seven thousand sheep, three thousand camels, five hundred yoke of oxen, five hundred female donkeys, and a very large exquisite household. As we can see Job was truly blessed. To break it down Job had seven thousand sheep. I am sure that his family wore the best of clothes because sheep produces wool.

The three thousand camels in those days and times they were top of the line transportation. In our time it's considered Corvettes, Nissan Maxima, Toyota Avalon's, and Hummers. As far as the five hundred oxen and female donkeys, this represented that Job possessed heavy machinery. The female donkeys plowed, carried grains and harvest from the fields. The oxen pulled and pushed trees and rock boulders. Also oxen produced good meats such as steaks, ribs, and hamburger as well.

Knowing Your Identity

Job was really blessed as you can see and it was all because of Gd. When God blesses us in all areas an aspects of our lives the enemy which is Satan don't like it. One day Satan shook his head from side to side and said "It's time that I attack Job. He's living too good," Now I didn't hear Satan say this but I know how he operates. Anytime you're walking and living in good orderly direction, which is the true route of God, beware Satan is coming. Let's take a look at verses 6-12.

Verse 6: Now there was a day when the sons of God came to present themselves before the Lord, and Satan came among them.

Verse 7: And the Lord said to Satan, "From where do you come?" So Satan answered the Lord and said, "From going to and from on the earth and walking back and forth on it."

Verse 8: Then the Lord said to Satan, "Have you considered my servant Job, that there is none like him on the earth, a blameless and upright man, and one who fears God and shun evil?"

Verse 9: So Satan answered the Lord and said, "Does Job fear God for nothing?"

Verse 10: Have you not made a hedge around him, around the household, and around all that he has on every side?" You have blessed the work of his hands, and his possessions have increased the land.

Verse 11: "But now, stretch out your hand and touch all that he has, and he surely curse you to your face!"

Knowing Your Identity

Verse 12: And the Lord said to Satan, "Behold all that he has is in your power; only do not lay a hand on his person," so Satan went out from the presence of the Lord.

As you can see before Satan could attack Job he has to ask God for permission. That shows Satan has no power. He's the ruler of the world; Satan can only attack material possessions, financial issues, sickness, and family matters. It's all an attack on the mind. There's a flip side to it though. If God is in charge of your destiny know that no weapon formed against you shall prosper.

Satan attacked Jobs' oxen because of his spirit rising up in the Sabean tribe, which also killed Job servants as well. Through fire Satan also attacked and killed Job's sheep and also most of his servants. The Chaldean tribe came through and raided Job's camels and also killed the servants that groomed and fed them. Also a great wind came and struck the house and killed Job's children. Just that fast Job lost his oxen.

In those days oxen did the work of bull-dozer, caterpillar, forklift, and tractors. Job lost all of his heavy machinery. He lost his fine selections of meat too. The sheep that he lost was just as if he'd lost his own brand name clothing. Also...as far as his camels being raided, Job lost his car industry; Then...on the count, of a great wind killing his children, as a hurricane does, at this day and time.

Let me ask you a question? If you were in Job's shoes how would you feel? Well...that wasn't the end of it. You have to go on a read the whole book. Satan...the devil himself, continued to come at him. He caused boils to also form

Knowing Your Identity

all over Job's body. Satan is a spirit. He even got inside of Job's wife. Causing her to say due to stress and anxiety; especially….after the fame was gone.

Chapter 2 verse 9."Do you still hold fast to your integrity? Curse God and die! No matter what Satan had took from Job, even after what his wife had said. Job still stood up for God.

The storm passed and it was a new day in Job's life. Everything that he lost was restored and more was added by God. In life we're going to be tested by the enemy. We must hold on and keep our faith in God. Job knew his identity as far as being strong. Always knowing who we are, as far as children of God, gives us total confidence that no matter what, Satan brings our way, we're going to make it through. We were built for storms. It's a part of our identity. A true fact. If God is for us, who can be against us? Just know it's only a test you're going through. It's going to be over real soon. Keep the faith. Don't give up!

Knowing Your Identity

Chapter 10

Being Redeemed

Isaiah Chapter 43, Verses 1-7

This segment is for the ones who are struggling as far as knowing their identity as a child of God. These are people who grew up in the church, sung on the choir, were an active member and participant in all church activities and functions. But for some reason walked away or strayed away. Even though this happen doesn't mean that the love for God isn't in their heart. God knows this and that's why he is called the redeemer, the same one left ninety nine sheep to go get one, yes that same one sheep that was lost.

In some churches today a lot of congregations seem to forget the lost. As long as attendance rate is up to par, money is coming in, nice cars are being driven, nobody needs or ask for help the church is doing fine. So if they lose a sheep it doesn't matter. Well that's not Gods way and how he operates. God operates out of love and because of that love he possess he can't go without that one. Due to Satan coming after the church he catches a lot of God's children off guard in their teenage days. Peer pressure in school comes there way and causes them to get off track and the next thing you know they're no longer attending church.

Satan also attacks the older generation. He'll cause financial situations to get out of hand and they'll be forced to work hours on their job on Sundays which separates them from church. Some people inherits sickness, that causes them to become bedridden, crippled or even hospitalized to the point of they can't attend church anymore. The whole scenario about this is that these people don't get

Knowing Your Identity

phone calls, visits, letters or cards from the church saying they are missed and everything will be alright.

It's all a part of the redeeming system of God. Leaving ninety nine sheep to go get one is what we are supposed to do.

Let's take a look at Isaiah chapter 43 verses 1-7. This will show what God says he'll do to go out and redeem his people.

Verse 1: But now thus said the Lord, who created you, O'Jacob, and he who formed you, O Israel: Fear not, for I have redeemed you; I have called you by your name; you are mine.

Verse 2: When you pass through waters, I will be with you; And through the rivers, they shall not overflow you. When you walk through fires you shall not be burned. Nor shall a flame scorch you.

Verse 3: For I am the Lord your God, the Holy One of Isreal, your savior; I gave Egypt for your ransom, Ethiopia and Seba in your place.

Verse 4: Since you was precious in my sight, you have been honored, And I have loved you; therefore I will give men for you, and people for your life.

Verse 5: Fear not for I am with you; I will bring your descendants from the east, and gather you from the west;

Verse 6: I will say to the north, "Give them up" and to the south, "Don't keep them back!" Bring my sons from afar. And my daughters from the end of the earth.

Knowing Your Identity

Verse 7: Everyone who is called by my name, whom I created for my glory; I have formed him, yes I have made him."

This is how God goes out and get his lost sheep. That is how we are supposed to display our identity. People who has walked away from the church needs that kind of love. Showing them that we love and miss them. That really gives them the inspiration to bounce back and realize their identity as far as being a child of God.

In life even though we go to church a lot of us inherit different phases of difficult situations.

These situations causes us to say this church stuff isn't working. That's what the devil wants us to thing. The devil don't care how much you go to church, or how good you can sing, the nice suits or dresses that we were, and especially the sermon that we heard. None of that is a threat to him, if we don't learn anything. It's so very important that we learn our faith in God as far as our identity.

God has known each and every last one of us, from our mother's womb, and he's named and called each and every one of us to do his will. If you are that one sheep who's been through a lot, after walking away from church, doesn't it feel good to be redeemed? It must feel good if you're back sitting in the congregation at church after being sick, or bedridden because of sickness. It shows that you are anointed and God always go out and get his anointed.

Well we go through situations that will try to wipe us out, and cause us to feel unworthy and walk away from the church. It's not about what we go through.

It's how we come out. That's because of the true power and love of God. He's the Redeemer!

Knowing Your Identity

Chapter 11

Shaped and Molded

Jerimiah Chapter 18 Verses 1-6

Verse 1: A message came to me from the Lord. He said,

Verse 2: "Go down to the potter's house. I will give you my message there."

Verse 3: So I went down to the potter's house. I saw him working at his wheel.

Verse 4: His hands were shaping a pot out of clay. But he saw that something was wrong with it. So he formed it into another pot. He shaped it in a way that seemed best to him.

Verse 5: Then the Lord's message came to me. He said "People of Israel, I can do with you just as the potter does, "announces the Lord," The clay is in the potter's hand. And you are in my hand, people of Israel.

If clay could talk as it's being molded. I bet it would say "ouch" I imagine you being in the form of clay, and spinning on potter's wheel. As the potter digs his hands in you, shapes and molds you over and over again that wouldn't feel so good.

That's how we feel at times, when God shapes and molds us, not into how we choose to be but how he wants us to be. In church today as far as members are concerned everybody didn't have satisfactory lifestyle. Some of us have experienced some rough and difficult times. None of those difficult times was

Knowing Your Identity

never what we asked for; I remember in school in the first grade, my school teacher asked me what I wanted to be when I grow up? I said, "A doctor." Other kids in the class said astronaut, dentist, police, movie star, or an athlete.

When we said what we wanted to be it came from our hearts. Some of us live up to our dreams and some of us don't, and because of those tarnished dreams that dulled out the people of God find themselves working in restaurants, construction, and some don't even have a job, so they give up. Giving up for feeling short changed in life and that cause us to feel that God doesn't love us.

But I'm here to tell you that he does. In the kingdom of God we'll find ourselves experiencing hard times. It's all a part of being on the potter's wheel. God is forming us and shaping us into what he wants us to be. Even the feeling of being short changed in life, will cause us to get involved in street life, which bring drugs and alcohol to help cope with the situation.

Doing that eventually lands us as children of God in jail, prison, institutions, or even death. Standing in front of the school teacher when we were young none of us said we wanted to be short changed in life.

In life we may not understand why we inherit difficult situations at times. I'm here to tell you that is not by accident it's for a purpose. It's all for the glory of God. Each and every day I see God moving and also during a major turnaround in people lives. As I shared being on the potter's wheel hurts.

We may be working in a restaurant making minimum wages. With that type of pay rate we're just able to get by. On construction sites we may be working in the winter time and our pay checks don't add up to the pain we endure from the

Knowing Your Identity

cold weather. Still eventually we get by even though we can't find employment. Somehow God provides and the next thing you know we are employed.

These testimonies we share in church with others. As times goes by we find ourselves with better jobs, owning our own business, and living the life that we dreamed of when were young. We may not be astronaut, dentist, police, movie star, or an athlete, but we find ourselves living good as if we were. Life doesn't look as bad as it did. Am I right?

It is because God is the potter and he knows what's best for us. Being of the flesh when it comes to life situation, we try to mold and shape the issue as if we are the potter. All we do is make a mess out of the situation. God is the true potter and being in his hands is a true blessing. The situations that allow us to face only make us stronger and better people. All we have to do is let him guide us to a more better direction.

Always remember, let God do for us what we can't do for ourselves. No matter what has occurred in our lives, he'll always mold and shape us to be better than ever. God had true promises for us as far as our future hopes. He didn't bring us this far to leave us. Continue to let God be the potter in your life. You'll turn out to be a beautiful piece of art in society.

Knowing Your Identity

Chapter 12

We are Watchman

Ezekiel Chapter 3 Verses 17-21

Being watchman is part of our identity also. It's our duty to tell the people of God and of sin that God is so very powerful and awesome. We must also give them a little autobiography about our lives and what God has done for us. People who are caught up in sin may feel like that they are so low in life that God can't help them.

That's the way Satan wants them to feel and believe, but we know different. We know God loves us each and every last one of us, and he'll never leave or forsake us.

In this book of Ezekiel Chapter 3: 17-21. It tells us our duty as far as being a child of God. A lot of us in the church has a lot of ups and down in our lives. When we are up and on our feet, we must uplift others whether they doing good or bad. Let's take a look at these key verses that explains our duties as children of God.

Verse 17: "Son of man, I have made you a watchman for the house of Israel; therefore hear a word from my mouth; and give them warning for me:

Verse 18: When I say to the wicked. "You shall surely die" and you give him no warning, nor speak to warn the wicked from his wicked ways, to save his life that some wicked man shall die in his iniquity; but his blood I will require at your hand.

Knowing Your Identity

Verse 19: "Yet, if you warn the wicked and he does not turn from this wickedness, nor his wicked ways he shall die in his iniquity; but you have delivered your soul.

Verse 20: "Again when a righteous man turns from his righteousness and commits iniquity, and I lay a stumbling block before him, he shall die; because you did not give him warning, he shall die in his sin, and his righteousness which he has done shall not be remembered; but his blood I will require at your hand.

Verse 21: "Nevertheless if you warn the righteousness man that the righteous should not sin, he shall surely live because he took warning; also you will have delivered your soul."

Those are our duties in scripture that's laid out to us. Today we see people at the grocery stores, walking in the neighborhoods, on television, and even on our jobs telling us all about the king of kings and the Lord of Lords. Some people stand and listen, while others try to get away. Somehow the shepherd's words always find the sheep. Even though people may get caught up in sin, it's still our duty to give them the message of God and let them know that there's a better for them. God can and will supply their every need.

He can't supply their needs if the word is not given to them Sharing the word of God with people who are caught up in sin, can sometimes be just exactly what they wanted to hear. All they want to know is that somebody loves them, and there is a new way of life. We can't wonder what people look like or what they are going to day.

We have to walk up to them with faith and speak the work of God to them.

Knowing Your Identity

If you speak it to them and they receive it, you've delivered their soul and yours. That doesn't only causes angels to rejoice in heaven, it also causes God to bless us for bringing in a lost soul.

Now what happens if you're told by the spirit of God to share a word with a person who's of sin that you see drunk in a convenience store. Even though you were told by the spirit to share the word, still you say "No." They're not going to want to hear the word. Then you get in your car and leave. What happens once you get home and look at the 6'o' clock news and see that person was struck and killed by a car as she/he was trying to cross the street. So much for being a watchman. Their blood is on your hands. That would feel so bad wouldn't it?

As people of God our identity calls for us to be people of love, understanding, and composition. Even to the righteous person who's strayed away from the flock. It's our duty to let them know that the road of sin is total destruction and they need to come back to the pasture because God loves them. Normally when we as people of God backslide, it's because of a form of escape due to failed marriages, worldly issue, or some sort of anxiety.

Those are the weapons that Satan uses to cause us as people of God to walk away from the church. As I shared, being the watchman it's our duty to share the word with them and let them know that God is the way. He's the truth and the life. You never know the impact that the word of God can have on people's lives. So no matter what, as far as identity, we as people of God shall always be watchman. Never hold back from playing your position. God needs you to be true watchman and share his word.

Knowing Your Identity

Chapter 13

Have No Fear

Ezekiel Chapter 28 Verses 12-16

In this book we have been discussing our identity as far as being a child of God. Now I want to shift the focus to a word which is "identify." The definition of identify is so very important that we need to know the full meaning of this word.

Identify – To recognize as being a particular person or thing; prove to be the same; to connect closely; link. The reason I'm on this topic is because it's time that we allow the spiritual essence of God standards, Satan always set out to sabotage. This is where it all stops. Verses 12-16 of Ezekiel Chapter 28 will give us insight of this evil spirit who tries to tear us down.

Verse 12: "Son of man, take up a lamentation for the king of Tyre, and say to him, "Thus says the Lord God, "You were the seal of perfection, full of wisdom and perfect in beauty.

Verse 13: You were in Eden, the garden of God; every precious stone was your covering; The sardius, topaz, diamond, beryl, onyx, jasper, sapphire, turquoise, and emerald with gold. The workmanship of your timbrels and pipes was prepared for you on the day you were created.

Verse 14: "You were the anointed cherub who covers; I established you; You were on the holy mountain of God; you walked back and forth in the mist of fiery stones.

Knowing Your Identity

Verse 15: You were perfect in your ways from the day you were created, until iniquity was found in you.

Verse 16: by the abundance of your trading you became violet within, and you sinned; therefore I cast you as a profane thing out of the mountain of God: And I destroyed you, O covering cherub, from the midst of the fiery stones.

It says it all in the scripture of Ezekiel 28 that you've just read. As you can see Satan known as Lucifer was once in heaven.

He was such a beautiful angel God made. The sardius, topaz, diamond, beryl, onyx, jasper, sapphire, turquoise, and emerald with gold, were pearly gates of heaven where Satan resided with God. He made music with the timbrel and pipes which was told in the scriptures. Because of the powerful influential vibe of music Satan which at the time was Lucifer began to think and say that he was God.

As we know there is only one God. Because of Lucifer's behavior in verse 16 it shows he was cast out of heaven. In the book of Luke Chapter 10 Verse 18, this is a cross reference to Ezekiel Chapter 28 verse 16. Luke Chapter 10 Verse 18: "And he said to them, "I saw satan fall like lightening from heaven."

That's what happened to Satan when he betrayed God. He was cast out of heaven faster than lightening. Imagine how fast lightning strikes. Just that fast Satan landed on the earth. When he hit the earth also came the spirt of lying, stealing, drug addition, alcoholism, murder, and all other sorts of negative things that are not of God. His job is to keep the people of God in bondage due to sin.

Knowing Your Identity

We can't allow that, and that's why we must be able to identify how he works. In verse 14 we see that God says that he established Satan. If we are of God Satan may come at us but he won't prosper at what he sets out to do. It says in the scripture. I've always been a person who loves to look at the news. I've seen people who have had tragedies happened to them due to violence, hurricanes, and car accidents. For some reason they always say "God why did you do this?"

I'm here to tell you that none of those tragedies is Gods' fault, they come from satan trying to make God look bad and have people blame him for the bad times. God is the one who works it all out. He's the one to call on when times are hard and rough. He's the doctor to all our problems and situations. We as children of God have to know that Satan is already defeated in all areas of our lives. Being in bondage a lot of people get caught up in music and lyrics about getting high, killing, and calling women out of their names, and using many curse words.

For some unknown reason the youth picks up on the kind of music and then it becomes a part of their everyday routine. It's because Satan uses communication. Even on the news they make ratings by tragic stories, such as killings, burnings, abductions, because nobody would watch the news if there's no bad thinks to report on. That's how the world is and this is Satan's' territory. If we stand for God and do all that's asked of us. Just like he did we'll also be able to cast Satan away from us as fast as lightning. Notice when we are doing God's will, Satan will come at us from all angles especially if you're in sin. Why? Because... you're already into his hall of fame. He doesn't have to go after you if he's already got you.

Knowing Your Identity

Come out before it's too late. God is always waiting for us to call upon him to pull us out of bondage. All we have to do is call upon his name. Seeing the scripture and hearing all that I'm sharing with you is pure truth. The devil is no match for God when he comes at you, have no fear because God has already defeated him. Just know and believe that you possess all powers for the victory. I speak from experience because I've seen the works of God. He will give you the spiritual essence to identify Satan.

Knowing Your Identity

Chapter 14

Shepherd and Sheep

Ezekiel Chapter 34 Verses 11-14

The word shepherd you heard me use that term in this book retaining to God. Being children of God we are considered to be his sheep also. Previously in this book I also talked about being called by God from our mother's womb. For some reason as sheep we at times will stray away from the pasture. That pasture that I'm talking about is our walk with God.

Let's take a look at Ezekiel Chapter 34 Verse 11-14. This will give us a much better outlook as far as how God goes all out to get his children who's strayed away from the posture.

Verse 11: For thus says the Lord God: "Indeed I myself will search for my sheep and seek them out."

Verse 12: "As a shepherd seeks out his flock on the day he is among his scattered sheep, so will I seek out my sheep and deliver them from all the places where they were scattered on a cloudy and dark day.

Verse 13: "And I will bring them out from the people and gather them from the countries, and I will bring them there to their own land; I will feed them on the mountain of Israel, in the valleys and in all the inhabited places of the country.

Knowing Your Identity

Verse 14: "I will feed them good pasture, and their fold shall be on the high mountains of Israel, There they shall lie down in a good fold and feed in the rich pasture on the mountains of Israel.

As we can see verses 11-14 makes a tremendous statement. If you are the sheep of his flock and strayed away you can count on it God is coming. Over in Scotland when shepherds discovered that one of their sheep strayed away they couldn't reset until they found that sheep. There was no mountain to high, no river to wide or no valley that was too low. They were on a mission to find their prize possession.

This may sound harsh but once a shepherd finds the sheep they would pop the sheep on his hind leg as a form of chastisement. After the chastisement was initiated the shepherd would pick up the sheep and carry it back to the pasture. Once that sheep gets back to the pasture it never leaves again,

That's how God operates. Being children of God as I shared at times we stray away from the pasture normally it's due to curiosity. At times we may feel that this Christian life is so boring and we feel that a little adventure needs to be added. I have a much scenario that will give you better insight. I met a young man one time and he shared with me about how curiosity caused him to take a step out of the pasture. The young man said his life revolved around church.

His parents were active members and by this he was always there also. At all church functions such as, deacon board meetings, choir rehearsals, etc. and doing activities all the time with the church. The young man also shared the fact that as far as school he couldn't dress like other kids. Other kids his age was wearing

Knowing Your Identity

sweat suits, jeans, nautical shirts, Nike and air force one shoes. The young man wore dress shirts, slacks, and dress shoes.

This caused him to be singled out and teased a lot. In these children eyes and at school all this young man said is that he wanted was acceptance. Curiosity got the best of him and caused him to take a sep away from the pasture, and rebel against his parents spiritual rituals. He no longer went to church, or church functions, dress close he no longer wore. He became of the world entertaining so called friends who cared very little about him. He began to hang out in the streets which led to jail and prison. Do you see what curiosity did?

It's good to have God in our lives. Being the shepherd God went out and got his sheep. The young man shared the fact that when he was of the world it seemed everywhere he went there was someone telling him about God. He also shared that Christian people who he came across as he ran the streets would often say to "Son I can feel that you are one of God's children. You need to get yourself back in church. They didn't even know this young man and he continue to ignore them.

Suddenly, he found himself in jail and on the way to prison. In the prison he said a pastor who volunteered at the facility seen him at a service and said "Son come on back to the pasture" The prison is a form of chastisement because you know better.

Being a child of God who strayed away from the pasture he suddenly started to remember his identity. Today he's back in church and doing very well. Even though God found his sheep in prison he is still back in the pasture. Leaving the

Knowing Your Identity

pasture due to curiosity is very dangerous for us because Satan is the wolf and he chooses to eat us up. That's why it's so important of knowing who and who's we are. We're so blessed to have God in our lives as our shepherd. That's why we need to stay in the pasture so we can't go wrong.

Knowing Your Identity

Chapter 15

Through the Fire

Daniel Chapter 3 Verse 1-27

As children of God we go through a lot in life. Storms and situations seems so impossible to overcome. Still somehow we come out of them. That power to overcome those tough situations comes from God. I want us together to look at the book of Daniel.

Chapter 3 verse 1-27 it tells us about three men who were dedicated to God. Their names were Shadrach, Meshach, and Abednego. They went through a major experience with the king Nebuchadnezzar that could've cost them death. But, by loving and believing in God, with the greatest of faith, they made it out a very tough and difficult situation. Let's look now at a few key scriptures in the book of Daniel. This experience that Shadrach, Meshach, and Abed-nego went through will show you how God comes through at the last moment to save his children.

Verse 1: Nebuchadnezzar the king made an image of gold, whose height was sixty cubits and its width was six cubits. He set it up in the plain of Dura, in the province of Babylon.

Verse 2: And king Nebuchadnezzar sent word to gather together satraps, the administrators, the governors, the counselors, the treasures, the judges, the magistrates, and all the officials of the provinces, to come to the dedication of the image which king Nebuchadnezzar had set up.

Knowing Your Identity

Verse 3: so the satraps, the administrators, the governors, the counselors, the treasurers, the judges, the magistrates, and all the officials of the provinces gathered together for the dedication of the image that king Nebuchadnezzar had set up; and they stood before the image that Nebuchadnezzar had set up.

The king is powerful as we can see. He built a statue out of pure gold and he called all people of power to come and look at it. Not only did he show them the statue, he also gave them a command.

Verse 4: Then a herald cried aloud "To you it is commanded, O people, nation, and languages.

Verse 5: "That at the time you hear the sound of the horn, flute, harp, lyre, and psaltery, in symphony with all kinds of music, you shall fall down and worship the gold image that king Nebuchadnezzar had set up.

Verse 6: And whoever doesn't fall down and worship shall be cast immediately into the midst of the burning fiery furnace. Now as you read the kings commands how do you feel? This threat was sent to all including the administrators, the governors, the counselors, the treasurers, the judges, the magistrates, and all the officials of the provinces which we know today as the big time people.

Even though they had power they still obeyed because they knew that the king had more. They also knew that by not bowing down to the statue king Nebuchadnezzar had set up, it would be death. As we see the king has taken his power to the extreme.

Knowing Your Identity

Verse 7: So at the time, when all of the people heard the sound of the horn, flute, harp and lyre in symphony, with all kinds of music, all the people, nations, and languages, fell down and worshiped the gold image that king Nebuchadnezzar had set up. These people of power were forced to serve a false god. They were in a touch position due to certain pressures of life. Dealing with the flesh we find ourselves just going along with the programs of Satan. I'm about to show you how Shadrach, Meshach and Abednego stuck with God's true program. They only knew and believed in one God, nothing and nobody, not even the king, could cause them to bow down to his statue. Let's look at.

Verse 12: "There are certain Jews whom you have set over the affairs of the province of Babylon: Shadrach, Meshach and Abednego; these men, O king, have not paid due regard to you. They don't serve your gods or worship the gold image which you have set up."

Verse 13: Then Nebuchadnezzar, in rage and fury gave command to bring Shadrach, Meshach and Abednego. They brought these men before the king.

The rest of the chapter you have to read. Being true children of God Shadrach, Meshach and Abednego still refuse to bow down to the statue. They also told Nebuchadnezzar that to his face and in front of all the people. The king ordered them to be thrown into the fiery furnace seven times hotter. The soldiers followed the king's command and they tossed Shadrach, Meshach and Abednego fiery furnace. As time went by the king felt something was wrong because there wasn't any hollering or the smell of human flesh burning. The king took a look in the furnace.

Knowing Your Identity

Verse 24-25; then king Nebuchadnezzar was astonished; he rose in haste and spoke saying to his counselors "Did we not cast three men bound into the mist of the fire?" They answered and said to the king. "True, O king."

Verse 25: "Look!" He answered "I see four men loose walking in the midst of the fire; and they are not hurt. And the form of the fourth is the son of God."

That's how God works it out. He may not come when we want him but he's right on time. In life we go through fires regarding situations and by the power of God we come out of the fire without the smell of smoke on us. Aren't you glad that we don't look like what we've been through? Just like Shadrach, Meshach and Abednego, we must always know our identity. In life we don't have to sell ourselves short by following and bowing down to false gods. On our side we have God, the true power, and we must always give him the glory for bringing us through the fire.

Knowing Your Identity

Chapter 16

Being Tempted

Matthew – Chapter 4

Verses 1 – 11

The topic "Being Tempted" that I'm about to elaborate on is what happens to us each and every day. Living on earth we know that this is Satan's world and he stays busy. Jesus the son of God was also tested by Satan. In the desert forty days and forty nights on a fast, the devil comes at us. He comes when we feel hopeless from the fierce blows that the world hits us with because of Satan.

In the book of Matthew verses 1-11, we are going to see just how Satan operates. If he came at the son of God to steal, kill, and destroy. Imagine what he sets out to do to us. Let's new look at verses 1-11.

Verse 1: Then Jesus was led up by the spirit into the wilderness to be tempted by the devil.

Verse 2: And when he had fasted forty day and forty nights, afterward he was hungry.

Verse 3: Now when the tempted came to him, he said, "If you are the Son of God, command that these stones become bread."

Knowing Your Identity

Verse 4: But he answered and said, "It is written, Man shall not live by bread alone, but by every word that proceeds from the mouth of God."

Verse 5: then the devil took him up into the holy city, set him on the pinnacle of the temple.

Verse 6: and said to him, "If you are the son of God, throw yourself down. For it is written: He shall give his angels charge over you, and, in their hands they shall bear you up. Lest you dash your foot against a stone."

Verse 7: Jesus said to him, "It is written again, you shall not tempt the Lord your God."

Verse 8: Again, the devil took him up on an exceedingly high mountain, and showed him all the kingdoms of the world and their glory.

Verse 9: And he said to him, "All these things I will give you if you will fall down and worship me."

Verse 10: Then Jesus said to him, "Away with you, Satan! For it is written, "You shall worship the Lord your God, and him only you shall serve."

Verse 11: Then the devil left him, and behold, angels came and ministered to him.

As you can see we must always be on guard. From these scriptures we see that the devil is busy. Now you've heard in verse three the word "Tempter" used. Satan has many names. He's called the devil, the deceiver, tempter, also has called the prince of darkness. His job is to come at us, children of God, and

Knowing Your Identity

do all that he can to turn us away from God. In these scriptures as you can see he tried to do the something to Jesus. The key words to what I just said were "he tried."

As we see, it didn't work. It's because Jesus, no matter how weak he was at the time, was deep and rooted in the word. Be mindful now Jesus was the word in the flesh. Being of the flesh fasting forty days and forty nights, can you imagine how he felt? Imagine how we feel when we haven't eaten in a few hours, we find ourselves either stopping at the nearest restaurant, or raiding the refrigerator as soon as we got home. It's because in our minds we were hungry. That's how the devil operates by the mind. Look at the manipulation skills that he played with Jesus mind. That's what he does to us. He comes at us, children of God harder than ever, to detour us from walking with God. That's why we must be and stay deep and rooted in Christ.

Being the tempter the devil will definitely come as us while we are fasting. Notice as you begin you fast suddenly a lot of food commercials will begin to come over the television. As you are driving you'll notice bill board advertisements about McDonald's, Bo Jangles, or Golden Corral. For some reason they all sticks out at us.

The devil will whisper to you, "Break your fast. Go on get you something to eat. God don't care.

Those are the mind games that he plays. That's not all that he does. He tells smart kids in school, "It's alright to get high. Once they do they eventually drop out of school.

Knowing Your Identity

Satan even convinces kids to join gangs, which causes them to go to jail or prison. Some eventually get killed. On jobs satan tells "us" Forget your boss. You don't have to take his orders. Just quit. Go on ahead and walk out of the door."

Be aware Satan also goes to church. In the church he's the "author of confusion." He creates gossip. Such gossip as who things they are the best singer in the chair. Also who has on the most expensive dress or suit, there should not be competition in the church. We are all there to be united in the body of God.

Drama in the church comes from Satan. It's all mind games. This scripture gives us insight of his tricks. Remember we discussed that Satan was once a powerful angel in heaven? Just like Jesus, he knows the word of God too. Just like Jesus shot scriptures at Satan in the desert. So did Satan shoot the word at Jesus? Jesus's word was powerful and that's why he caused the devil to flee. Just like Jesus when we are tempted, and he'll flee. It's all a part of our identity as children of God to be tempted.

Knowing Your Identity

Chapter 17

Perfectly Insured

Matthew – Chapter 9

Verses 23-27

There are 66 books in the bible. The Old Testament has 39 books in it. In the New Testament it features 27 books. I want us to take a look at the word testament. The word testament stands for a contract, agreement, a band, or a vow. That goes to show that God word is a true vow from his heart. The bible gives us good orderly directions. God's word will never mislead us. With his word we are also perfectly insured if we live accordingly to God's blueprint to life.

In our walk with God at times things get a little hectic from everyday life. Bills pile up on us, which causes economic problems to out weight our tolerance span. It seems at times that whatever you do on your job isn't good enough in your boss's eyes. Even at home at times we find ourselves never having time to wind down and rest because of carrying the fort. These types of feelings my cause us to say, "Where is Jesus at? This is not how a Christian life is supposed to be."

I'm here to tell you, "Welcome to the Christian life." This chapter will show you that no matter what storms come your way you are perfectly insured. In the book of Matthew chapter 9 verses 23-27 and find out.

Verse 23: Now when he got into a boat, His disciples followed him.

Knowing Your Identity

Verse 24: And suddenly a great tempest arose on the sea, so that the boat was covered with the waves. But he was asleep.

Verse 25: Then his disciples came to him and awoke him saying, "Lord save us! We are perishing!"

Verse 26: But he said to them, "Why are you fearful, O you of little faith?" Then he arose and rebuked the winds and the sea, and there was a great calm.

Verse 27: So the men marveled, saying, "Who can this be, that even the winds and the sea obey him."

As you can see in the scriptures the disciples didn't believer that they were perfectly insured. Jesus had done all of these miracles before their eyes, as they followed him.

To share the spotlight with Jesus makes us stars. As you can see the disciples loved being under to spotlight with Jesus as he catered to everybody who had sort of a crisis in their lives. They even followed him on a boat.

Being on the boat with Jesus, the disciples had a little crisis of their own.

It says in verse 2 that a tempest arose on the sea to the point that waves covered the boat. The disciples were wide awake while Jesus was asleep. All that Jesus done that day being of the flesh, I'm sure that he was tired. Let's take a look at the word also in verse 2 "Tempest." The definition of "Tempest" is: A violent wind storm.

Knowing Your Identity

Not only were the waves covering the boat, they were also rocking it too. Being also that waves are of water. I'm sure water was getting into the boat. Remember. A tempest is a violent windstorm. While the disciples were losing despair, Jesus was asleep. Can you imagine that? Picture this. The disciples looking at all that's going on because of this violent windstorm and then looking over at Jesus. Let me take you back to something that I said a few lines back.

"Being on the boat with Jesus, the disciples had a little crisis of their own."

I say little because this violent windstorm which was so called a tempest was a very small thing to Jesus.

In verse 25, it shows that the disciples feared death and they couldn't take it no more. And they quickly wake Jesus up.

In verse 26, once Jesus was awake, he looked at the disciples and said, "Why are you fearful, O you of little faith?" Then he arose and calmed the storm. As you can see the wind and waves obey Jesus.

So this is what these scriptures tell us. The world may rock us financially as we are trying to make ends meet. On our jobs it may get a little hectic. Sickness may arise in our lives. At times it may seem that nothing is working out. I just want you to know don't lose hope or get caught up in anxiety. On this boat of the world, you are not alone. Jesus is with you. Waves of the world may rock us. Winds of the world may try to knock us down. Just call on Jesus and he'll calm all of our storms. In our identity as far as children of God we'll always be perfectly insured. It's a vow from God.

Knowing Your Identity

Chapter 18

Doing What's Right

Matthew – Chapter 27

Verses 31-45

Being children of God, during what's right shouldn't be a job. As far as our identity it should be a way of life. When I refer to doing what's right as a job, this is what I mean. Getting up in the morning to go to work isn't always a good feeling at all. We deal with traffic jams, and also deal with meeting our quota, as we all know, that can be hectic at times. When it comes to doing what's right, it should never feel like a job. It should be a task that makes us feel good all over. I say this because in life we deal with people who are so very less fortunate than we are. A lot of those people need help. I'm speaking of homeless people. Some who are sick and even people who are in jails, and prisons. A lot of churches just basically focus on who's in attendance. What about the people who are caught up in some of life's most difficult situations. Doing what's right we must always help these type of people by the word of God. Let's take a look at the book of Matthew Chapter 27 verses 31-45. These scriptures give us a more insight as far as how we should as children of God, reach out to those who are less unfortunate.

Verse 31: "When the son of man comes in his glory, and all the holy angels with him, then he will sit on the throne of his glory.

Knowing Your Identity

Verse 32: "All the nations will be gathered before him, and he will separate them one from another, as a shepherd divides his sheep from the goats.

Verse 33: "And he will set the sheep on his right hand, but the goats on the left.

Verse 34: "Then the king will say to those on his right hand, "Come, you blessed of my father, inherit the kingdom prepared for you from the foundation of the world:

Verse 35: "For I was hungry and you gave me food; I was thirsty and you gave me drink; I was a stranger and you took me in;

Verse 36: I was naked and you clothed me; I was sick and you visited me; I was in prison and you came to me.

Verse 37: "then the righteous will answer Him saying, 'Lord, when did we see you hungry and feed you, or thirsty and give you a drink?

Verse 38: 'When did we see you a stranger and take you in, or naked and clothe you?

Verse 39: 'Or when did we see you sick, or in prison, and come to you?

Verse 40: 'And the king will answer and say to them, Assuredly, I say to you, inasmuch as you did it to one of the least of these my brethren, you did it to me.

Knowing Your Identity

Verse 41: "Then he will also say to those on the left hand, "Depart from me, you cursed, into the everlasting fire prepared for the devil and his angels:

Verse 42: 'For I was hungry and you gave me no food; I was thirsty and you gave me no drinks;

Verse 43: "I was a stranger and you did not take me in, naked and you did not clothe me, sick and in prison and you did not visit me.'

Verse 44: "Then they will answer him, saying "Lord, when did we see you hungry or thirsty, or a stranger or naked or sick or in prison, and did not minister to you?"

Verse 45: "Then he will answer them, saying, 'Assuredly, I say to you, inasmuch as you did not do it to one of the least of these, you did not do it to me."

As I shred, it's all about doing what's right. In the body of Christ we must have charity in our hearts. Today as far as the church we just focus on who's in our circle. What about people whose struggling outside of the church? When a church has a good and effective outreach program it causes the angels in heaven to rejoice. It also means that the church is bearing fruit. When a church is bearing fruit that means that the fruit is good and everybody wants to eat from that tree. What I mean by bearing fruit is, the church is spreading the word of God to hospital, homeless shelters, the streets, rehabilitation centers, jails, and also prisons, when we spread the word not only does the church grow but, it causes us to be blessed too. When we don't help people by reaching out, our tree doesn't bear fruit. That means that the church isn't putting out the word of

Knowing Your Identity

God as they should. They are just focused on delivering the word to their members. God doesn't like that. He wants us to bear fruit. That's what these scriptures verses 31-45 are teaching us. If people are hungry feed them, If people are thirsty give them a drink. If people need clothes, clothes them. If someone comes to you who is homeless, see what the church can do to find them shelter. If people are in the hospital sick, or incarcerated in jail or prisons go visit them, and take them the message of God. It helps us and also the church grow. In the church an outreach program is so very necessary. It's not all about us knowing our identity. We must also help other people in difficult situations realize their identity as well as far as being a child of God.

Knowing Your Identity

Chapter 19

Break through

Mark – Chapter 5

Verse 25-34

Together I want us to look at the definition of the word breakthrough.

Breakthrough – An out of overcoming or penetrating an obstacle of restriction. 2. A major success that permits further progress.

In life when situations get rough all we as children of God have to do is hold on. She had a menstruation period. The blood flowed from her for twelve years. All over the land she'd heard about a man by the of Jesus. She heard about him healing the sick, raising the dead, giving the blind sight, the deaf hearing, telling people who was paralyzed to walk again, and also casting out demons, the word was out about Jesus. Today he was in her town. Let's take a look at scriptures 25-34 and see what took place.

Verse 25: Now a certain woman had a flow of blood for twelve years,

Verse 26: and he suffered many things from many physicians. She had spent all that she had and was no better, but rather grew worse.

Verse 27: When she heard about Jesus, she came behind him in the crowd and touched his garment.

Knowing Your Identity

Verse 28: For she said, "If only I may touch his garment, I shall be made well."

Verse 29: Immediately the fountain of her blood was dried up, and she felt in her body that she was healed of the affliction.

Verse 30: And Jesus, immediately knowing in himself that power had gone out of him, turned around in the crowd and said, "Who touched my clothes?"

Verse 31: But his disciples said to him, 'You see the multitude thronging you and you say, "Who touched me?"

Verse 32: And he looked around to see her who had done this thing.

Verse 33: But the woman, fearing and trembling knowing what had happened to her, came and fell down before him and told him the truth.

Verse 34: And he said to her, "Daughter, your faith has made you well. Go in peace, and he healed of your affliction.

As you can see even though it took twelve years, the women continued to hold on by faith. Imagine blood flowing from us for twelve years. Just a loss of blood for 10 to 15 minutes causes us to get dizzy. This woman was supposed to have been dead a long time ago. It's by the power of God that she was still living. That word "power" is what causes a breakthrough. Imagine a person hitting a brick wall with a sledge hammer. In order to get a breakthrough it's going to take

Knowing Your Identity

a powerful swig. In that powerful swing, faith must be administered for a breakthrough.

With her faith, the woman took a very powerful swing at her brick wall, which was the blood flow of twelve years. Losing all of that blood, I'm sure that she was weak. Still... nothing was going to stop her from getting to Jesus. She had been dealing with this flow of blood for twelve years, and with the greatest of faith, she was determined, that today that nothing was going to hold her back, from getting healed.

We all know how Jesus was performing miracles across the land. Doing such miracles caused a great multitude of people with sicknesses, and other people who were just there to witnesses these miracles that Jesus performed.

Being weak because of the period of time which was twelve years, the woman still got up. Then she got dressed. She began with the greatest of faith to start her journey. In her mind was set that nothing, or nobody, was going to get in her way from Jesus. It's been a long time coming. And her breakthrough was due. Seeing the crowd which was gathered the sick, the blind, the deaf, the paralyzed, the dead, and the broken hearted. She knew that she had found Jesus and now this was her time. With determination, even though she was weak, still the woman walked her way through the crowd. She pushed and tagged even though she was weak. Finally once she made her way through the crowd, she layed eyes on Jesus. Seeing her Savior as tears flowed from her eyes, she knew that she's finally got her breakthrough. As she continued to approach Jesus, she said in verse 28, "If only I may touch his clothes I may be well."

Knowing Your Identity

Reaching out to Jesus and touching his clothes with the greatest of faith and determination the woman was healed. Immediately the fountain of her blood had dried up. She was now whole again because of her breakthrough. In life we may go through situations where we feel that we can't hold on. All we have to do is reach out to Jesus with the greatest faith. Eventually the dam that satan tries to build up in front of our progress will fall. Jesus is our sledge hammer to the difficult problems of life. We must always have the faith and determination to reach out to him. It took twelve years for the women to get a breakthrough. I know that twelve years is also a very long time. That's how Jesus get the glory. What a powerful testimony. Imagine a woman in church telling such a testimony as this, she was supposed to be dead. Still through it all, she's still very much alive, and in church testifying about the healing powers of Jesus. I've heard testimonies that were unbelievable.

I also know that there is nothing to impossible for Jesus to handle. Being of our identity as children of God, we make it through some of the most difficult situation. It's all because of the glory of God. People of God were once on life support and the doctors wanted to pull the plug. Also, people of God have lost jobs, and didn't know how they were going to make ends meet but, they somehow gets by. It's because of a breakthrough that is only administered by Jesus, our savior. Always know that we can depend on Jesus, to come through for us, no matter what the situation or circumstances are.

Knowing Your Identity

Chapter 20

Crucifixion

Matthew – Chapter 27

Verses 45-54

When Moses told Pharaoh to let his people go. Pharaoh didn't listen and we seen God give Moses the ability to cause plagues to happened all over Egypt. We've read in the bible how God flooded the earth in the time of Noah. How about in Sodom and Gomorrah? Remember, God caused fire and brimstone to rain down. All of this happened because of great and heinous sin. God doesn't like that. God being of love and compassion some way had to go about this in a different way. In those places where he caused plagues, floods, and fire and brimstone to rain down, being of God of love innocent people, not many through, was paying the price for other people's sins.

God knew this so he said "There's got to be a way that I don't punish the innocent for the guilty." God sought a way to come down to the earth in the flesh. He did just that. God became the word in the flesh. He did just that. God became the word in the flesh in the belly of Mary, who gave both to a baby boy whom she named Jesus. Being the word the flesh as Jesus grew up immediately he begun to teach and preach the message of God. He also showed people the power of God by performing miracles. We all know that he healed the sick. He caused the dead, gave the blind sight, and the deaf the ability to hear.

Knowing Your Identity

The spirit of God lived inside and outside of Jesus. He shared the word of God with each person that he'd come in the midst of. Each man or woman was now accountable for their own salvation. In God's eyes now as far as innocent people paying for the guilt's sin that issue was resolved. Now each person had the choice to choose their destiny, as far as their walk with God, or sin, which sin is to walk with Satan.

Because...of preaching and teaching the word of God, the Chief Priest's, the elders, and all of the council, began to arouse, and create controversy, which later produced sanctions for Jesus to be crucified. Let's take a look at the book of Matthew. Chapter 27 versus 45-54. This shows us what happened after the crucifixion.

Verse 45: Now for the sixth until the ninth hour there was total darkness over all of the land.

Verse 46: And about the ninth hour Jesus cried out with a loud voice, saying, "Eli, Eli, lama sabachthani? That is, "My God. My God. Why have you forsaken me?"

Verse 47: Some of those who stood there, when they heard that, said, "This man is calling for Elijah!"

Verse 48: Immediately...one of them ran, and took a sponge, filled it with sour wine, and put it on a reed, and offered it to him to drink.

Verse 49: The rest said, "Let him alone; let's see if Elijah will save him.

Knowing Your Identity

Verse 50: And Jesus cried out again with a loud voice, and yielded up his spirit.

Verse 51: Then behold, the veil of the temple was torn in two from top to bottom; and the earth quaked, and rocks were split.

Verse 52: And the graves were opened; and many bodies of saints who had fallen asleep were raised.

Verse 53: and coming out of the graves after his resurrection, they went into the holy city and appeared to many.

Verse 54: So…when the centurion and those with him, who were guarding Jesus, saw the earthquake, and things that had happened, they feared greatly, saying, "Truly…this was the son of God!"

Being children of God we are supposed to do his will by carrying and spreading the word. Jesus was sent on a mission for a purpose. The purpose was to deliver and set spirits free. By Jesus teaching and preaching the word, it created controversy, which later caused Jesus to be crucified.

In life as for as our identity, being children of God we also will inherit a crucifixion. I want to cross reference and go to the book of John Chapter 15 verse 4. This scripture gives us better insight as I speak about the crucifixions that we inherit. Listen to this in verse 4: "Abide in me, and I in you. As the branch cannot bear fruit of itself, unless it abides in the vine, neither can you, unless you abide in me.

Knowing Your Identity

The cross reference of John 15 verse 4 talks about abiding in Jesus Christ. Abiding in Christ is doing the will of God. In life doing the will of God will not always be peaches and cream. Being a child of God will also arouse controversy. We often find ourselves on the battlefield. Satan comes at us from all directions. Suddenly we are hit with all sorts of crisis. Family disputes, sicknesses, arise and causes us to take a fall. In some people's eyes we have been wrote off.

There's an opposite side to the crucifixion that happened to Jesus. Even though they whipped him, nailed him to the cross, and pierced his side. Jesus still rose from the dead. We have that same will power. It's in children of God's DNA. Look at all that we've been through in life because we abide in Jesus. His word says abide in me, and I in you. No matter how the devil comes at us with whatever kind of crucifixion well rise again. The devil had tried to break up our families. He's tried to tear us down with sicknesses. Because of following what's right we've even lost jobs. We've suffered financial burdens, and had near death experiences. As you can see, because we're still standing, that we continue to rise from all sorts of crucifixions. It's because of the will and glory of God. We'll always rise from crucifixions. It's in our identity to rise from the most impossible situations.

Knowing Your Identity

Chapter 21

Acts Chapter 9

Verses 1-20

Today's Damascus

In the book of Acts we e going to see how a man by the name of Saul, was filled with the evil spirit of Satan. If he seen or heard of anyone preaching, teaching, or even believing in the Lord Jesus Christ, he would inform the synagogues, that he knew that there were people, who weren't going by the teachings of Moses. Because...of them not following those teachings, they now followed the teachings of Jesus Christ.

This...Saul hated to the fullest. Towards the people who were following Jesus Christ he sent threats. Saul even brought warrants to arrest them. For some he sought death. If anybody was preaching, teaching, or believing in Jesus Christ were doomed.

As far as Saul's identity he was a very bad person. Can God use a person such as Saul, as an instrument for his word? Let's take a look at Acts Chapter 9 verses 1-20.

Verse 1: Then Saul, still breathing threats and murder, against the disciples of the lord, went to the High Priest.

Knowing Your Identity

Verse 2: and asked letters from him to the synagogues of Damascus, so that if he found any who were of the way, whether men or women, he might bring them bound to Jerusalem.

Verse 3: As he journeyed he came near Damascus, and suddenly a light shone around him from heaven.

Verse 4: Then he fell to the ground, and heard a voice saying to him," Saul, Saul, why are you persecuting me?"

Verse 5: And he said, "Who are you, Lord?" Then the Lord said," I'm Jesus, whom you are persecuting. It's hard for you to kick against the goads."

Verse 6: So, he trembling and astonished, said, "Lord...what do you want me to do?" Then the Lord said to him, "Arise... and go into the city, and you will be told what you must do."

Verse 7: And the men who journey with him stood speechless, hearing a voice but not seeing anyone.

Verse 8: Then Saul arose from the ground, and when his eyes were opened he saw no one. But they led him by the hand and brought him into Damascus.

Verse 9: And he was three day without sight, and neither at nor drank.

Verse 10: Now there was a certain disciple at Damascus named Ananias; and to him the Lord said in a vision, "Ananias." And he said, "Here I am Lord."

Knowing Your Identity

Verse 11: So the Lord said to him, "A rise and go to the street called straight, and inquire at the house of Judas for one called Saul of Tarsus, for behold, he is praying.

Verse 12: And in a vision he has seen a man named Ananias coming in and putting his hand on him, so that he might receive his sight."

Verse 13: The Aninias answered, "Lord, I have heard from many about this man, how much harm he has done to your saints in Jerusalem.

Verse 14: "And here he has authority from the chief priest to bind all who call on your name."

Verse 15: But the Lord said to him, "Go, for he is a chosen vessel of mine to bear my name before Gentiles, Kings, and the children of Israel.

Verse 16: For I will show him how many things that he must suffer for my names' sake."

Verse 17: And Ananias went his way and entered the house; and laying his hands on him he said, "Brother Saul, the Lord Jesus, who appeared to you on the road as you came, has sent me that you may receive your sight and be filled with the Holy Spirit."

Verse 18: Immediately there fell from his eyes something like scales, and he received his sight at once; and he rose and was baptized.

Verse 19: So when he had received food, he was strengthened. Then Saul spent some days with the disciples at Damascus.

Knowing Your Identity

Verse 20: Immediately he preached the Christ in the synagogues, that he is the Son of God.

As we can see, God can use anybody. Here Saul, who was full of the spirit of Satan, set out each and every day to persecute Christians. One day on the road to Damascus, which was on a day to do what he did best, and that was to seek Christians. Saul encountered more than what he bargained for. He was struck by a mighty light that caused him to lose his sight. The men who were a part of Saul's clan couldn't comprehend with what was going on. All they know is that Saul was knocked down, rubbing his eyes, and rolling around on the ground yelling. That's what happens when you mess with Gods children. Being blinded from this light was a true handicap to Saul. He was blind for three days. We all know that when times get hectic, and we can't stand the rain from the storms that life brings, we can always call on God and that's what Saul did.

Taking instructions from God, Saul was let into the city, as hje walked being led by his clan, people watched, some pointed, as we made he made his way to the house of Judah.

There was a prophet by the name of Ananias, who God told through the spirit, to go and lay hands on Saul, so that he may receive his sight.

Ananias said basically, "God this can't be you telling me this. This man lives to persecute Christians."

God said, "Go for he is a chosen vessel of mine to bear my name before Gentiles, kings, and the children of Israel."

Knowing Your Identity

From that point, Ananias took heed to the word of God. He went and laid hands on Saul. Once Saul received his sight by the healing powers of Jesus Christ, when worked through Ananias. From that point on Saul no longer went by his name. His name became Paul. By Ananias laying hands on him which restored his sight, Paul knew that the word and the powers of Jesus Christ were real. Coming out of such a handicap. Paul began to testify how he was once blind but now can see. Even though as Saul he persecuted Christians by the spirit of Satan. By being a chosen vessel of God, he now was Paul, and he was now converted to do the work of Jesus Christ. He rebuked demons. Paul carried the message thoroughly. He preached to the Romans, Galatians, Ephesians, Philippians, Colossians, Titus, and Philemon. When it come to the Corinthians, Thessalonians, and Timothy, the word was like honey in Paul's mouth that he had to tell them twice. Who would've ever thought that God would use Paul this way?

Just like today we see people who are involved in gangs, on drugs, are alcoholics, they want nothing to do with God. Those same people are who we walk away from. These are the people who God uses for his names sake. They are the ones who people point their fingers at and say. "They want amount to nothing, or be anything.

I'm here to tell you that God loves the underdog. I'm going cross reference again. In the book of Mark Chapter 10 verse 27 it says: But Jesus looked at them and said, "With men it is impossible, but not with God; for with God all things are possible."

Knowing Your Identity

People will think and have their minds made up, that a person can't change, or there is no hope for someone who is of the world. That's not the message that we are supposed to send by body language or words.

We are supposed to pray to God that he will change the person's lifestyle. Just as he did Paul. We all know that he was once a bad man. But nothing or nobody is to impossible for God to change. We must help people as children of God to learn their identity. They can change. Nobody is to impossible for God to change.

Knowing Your Identity

Chapter 22

We must Rejoice

Acts Chapter 9

Verses 25-31

Being children of God, our identity always calls for us to rejoice, no matter what circumstances are going on our lives. Being of the flesh at times, that can be so very hard to do. Imagine someone telling you to rejoice after you've just lost your job, and you've got bills to pay. How would you feel? I'm here to tell you that it's alright to rejoice because, we can upon Jesus Christ, and he'll restore all of that's lost. Speaking of rejoicing I want us to go to the book of Acts Chapter 9 verses 16-31. These scriptures will give us insight as far as rejoicing through difficult times. Paul and Silas encountered a difficult situation, which caused them to be locked up in prison, and facing a trial, which could cause them their lives, all because of preaching the word of Jesus Christ.

Verse 16: Now it happened, as went to prayer, that a certain slave girl possessed with a spirit of divination met us, who brought her masters much profit by fortune – telling.

Verse 17: The girl followed Paul and us, and cried out saying, "These men are the servants of the Most High God, who proclaim to us the way of salvation."

Knowing Your Identity

Verse 18: And this she did for many days. But Paul, greatly annoyed, turned and said to the spirit, "I command you in the name of Jesus Christ to come out of her." And he came out that very hour.

Verse 19 But when her masters saw that their hope of profit was gone, they seized Paul and Silas and dragged them into the marketplace to the authorities.

Verse 20: And they brought them to the magistrates, and said, These men, being Jews, exceedingly trouble our city;

Verse 21: And they teach customs which are not lawful for us, being Romans, to receive or observe."

Verse 22: Then the multitude rose up together against them; and the magistrates tore off their clothes and commanded them to be beaten with rods.

Verse 23: And when they has laid many strips on them, they threw them into prison, commanding the jailer to keep them securely.

Verse 24: Having received such a charge, he put them into the inner prison and fastened their feet in the stocks.

Verse 25: But at midnight Paul and Silas were praying and singing hymns to God, and the prisoners were listening to them.

Verse 26: Suddenly there was a great earthquake, so that the foundations of the prison were shaken; and immediately all the doors were opened and everyone's chains were loosed.

Knowing Your Identity

Verse 27: And the keeper of the prison, awaking from sleep and seeing the prison doors open. Supposing the prisoners had fled, drew his sword and was about to kill himself.

Verse 28: But Paul called with a loud voice, saying. "Do yourself no harm, for we are all here."

Verse 29: Then he called for a light, ran in, and fell down trembling before Paul and Silas.

Verse 30: And he brought them out and said, "Sir, what must I do to be saved?"

Verse 31: So they said, "Believe on the Lord Jesus Christ, and you will be saved, you and your household.

As we can see Paul and Silas was out in the region to do what they loved, preaching and teaching the word of Jesus Christ. We see in verse 16, a slave girl who was possessed by an evil spirit which was the spirit of Satan, began to follow them as they went to prayer.

Remember how we discussed in previous chapters of how the enemy comes at us. When it came to dealing with demon possessed people. Paul had zero tolerance. This went on for a many of days. Paul couldn't take it no more. He became annoyed and casted the demon out of the girl. In the name of Jesus.

The slave girl was a fortune teller and she brung her masters much profit from it. Now she no longer chose to be a fortune teller. Because of Paul

Knowing Your Identity

rebuking the evil spirit, she was made back whole. Her masters didn't like it, because fortune telling was their source of income. In verse 19; it shows that they became furious and seized Paul and Silas." Her masters then took them to the magistrates. And in verse 21: "And they teach customs which are not lawful for us, being roman, to receive or observe." They were speaking of the preaching and teachings of Jesus Christ. Because of this the multitude rose up against Paul and Silas and the magistrates tore their clothes off of them and whipped them. They were also thrown in jail. Still even though they sat in jail and didn't know whether their trail would cause them to die. Paul and Silas rejoiced as they still prayed and song hymns. Because they knew that their breakthrough was on the way. As they rejoice other prisoners listened and inside of their bodies registered true hope. True people of God, like Paul and Silas, know just how stir it up. Suddenly the earth quaked. The foundations of the prison were shaken loose. It was in the midnight hour that their breakthrough had arrived. With the work of God, as situations arise in our lives, we must rejoice, Because of rejoicing it caused the prison doors to also fly open. Prisoners were delivered and set free. The jailer was awaken and he seen the prison doors open. He called for a light, ran into dormitory, and fell down trembling before Paul and Silas. He seen that they were true dedicated men of Jesus Christ because, they didn't escape. The jailer asked as he felt the earthquake, seen the foundation of the prison leaning, and the chain locked doors open "what must I do to be saved?"

    In life, times may get hard situations may get difficult. It may seem like you can't go on. Just like Paul and Silas we must rejoice. As you know they rejoiced will not knowing what was going to take place as for as trial was concerned. Still they rejoice from that evening all the way into the midnight

Knowing Your Identity

hour. The spirit was stirred up. I don't know whether or not you know; But... at midnight it was a brand new day. We may be down one moment but rejoicing causes us to get up. In the spirit as far as children of God all we've got to do is show up and Jesus Christ will show out for us. That's why we must always rejoice.

Knowing Your Identity

Chapter 23

Our Ministry

2nd Corinthian's Chapter 6

Verses 1 – 10

The signs have taken place that its harvest time and Jesus is coming to gather his people. I have a question. Are you ready? I ask this because; in life we feel that we have time to make that decision. The truth is we don't. Nobody knows the time when Jesus will come. A lot of us who's been through a lot because of following Jesus Christ, preaches the word to people of the world, who think that they have time to make that decision. The people that I'm referring to are the ones who are of the world. These people are the ones who can have a major impact on others, by sharing testimonies, and preaching the word. I say this because they have major difficulties in their lives, and they can share their experiences, of all that they've been through. They can also share how God brung them out of those difficult situations. These people who I'm talking about have the ministry all over their lives. In 2nd Corinthians Chapter 6 verses 1-10. It talks about "Marks of the Ministry." Powerful people today of God have the marks. Let's take a look at what Paul says to the Corinthians. Nobody knows better than Paul we know how he felt about the word of Jesus Christ at first.

There is a flip side to everything in life. Look at how he was turned around. He also wanted others to know it's time to make that change! This is what he said.

Knowing Your Identity

Verse 1: We then, as workers together with him also plead with you not to receive the grace of God in vain.

Verse 2: For he says: "In an acceptable time I have heard you, and in the day of salvation I have helped you." Behold, now is the accepted time; behold now is the day of salvation.

Verse 3: We gave no offense in anything, that our ministry may not be blamed.

Verse 4: But in all things we commend ourselves as ministries of God: in much patience, in tribulations, in needs, in distresses,

Verse 5: In strips, in imprisonments, in tumults, in labors, in sleepless, in feelings.

Verse 6: by purity, by knowledge, by longsuffering, by kindness, by the holy spirit, by sincere love,

Verse 7: by the word of truth, by the power of God, by the armor of righteousness on the right hand and on the left.

Verse 8: by honor and dishonor, by evil report and good report; as deceivers and yet true;

Verse 9: As unknown, and yet well known; as dying and behold we live; as chastened, and yet not killed;

Knowing Your Identity

Verse 10: as sorrowful, yet always rejoicing; as poor, yet making many rich; as having nothing; and yet possessing all things.

If you've experienced those situations and somehow are still standing there's a ministry that resides inside of you. Let's look at the definition of ministry.

Ministry – 1. The act of serving; ministration. 2. The profession and services of minister 3. The building in which it is housed.

As we see that the ministry today has taking off and soared. I remember back in the days when ministers were rare. It was considered a boring and dull position. Today a lot of people have become ministers because of the love of God who causes them to want to change the world. Today there are also a lot of ministers out there of the world who God wants to use. We must get the message to them no matter where they are. These people need to know, that God has anointed them for one purpose, and one purpose only. The purpose is to love, preach, and teach the work of God. Their shortcomings from past lifestyles, backs up their walk and talk, because it was Jesus Christ who brings them out.

That's why it's important that we not look down on them. As ministers we must be of understanding. We must also share with them, not yesterday or tomorrow but, today is the day of salvation. Look at all that you've been through and for some reason you are still standing. The reason is Jesus. It's time that you take heed to the ministry that resides inside of you. If you are impatient, Jesus will deliver patience. Through tribulations, Jesus will bring comfort. In needs,

Knowing Your Identity

Jesus will deliver, and set us free. I just want you to get the point, of what lies inside of us, when it comes to our ministry. It's not about what it looks like. It's not about what it feels like. What it's all about is, how we come out of it. Take heed, you've been through the storm. Not it's time to come out. Please take heed to your ministry. It's time to deliver, and set spirits free, and let them know, how God has brung us out, of the many storms that we've endured. Take heed to your ministry because it's harvest time. It's all a part of our identity as children of God to share the ministry that's inside of us.

Knowing Your Identity

Chapter 24

Having Treasure

2nd Corinthians – Chapter 4

Verses 7 -15

In life children of God forget the treasure that we possess we are very fortunate to have this treasure. The treasure that I'm speaking of resides inside of us. I'm speaking of Jesus Christ. Jesus is the best treasure that anybody can find. Whatever, we ask of him will never come back as word. It's a blessing to have this treasure inside of us, especially when Satan brings a crisis our way. This treasure that we possess, you can cash in what I'm serving, because Jesus will allow us to continue to get back up. In 2nd Corinthians Chapter 4 verses 7-15. It tells us how we hit the jackpot, due to the treasures of Jesus Christ's spirit, living inside of us. Let's take a look at verses: 7-15.

Verse 7: But we have this treasure in earthen vessels that the excellence of the power may be of food and not of us.

Verse 8: We are hard pressed on every side, yet not crushed; we are perplexed, but not in despairs

Verse 9: Persecuted, but not forsaken; struck down, but not destroyed.

Verse 10: Always carrying about in the body the dying of the Lord Jesus, that the life of Jesus also may be manifested in our body.

Knowing Your Identity

Verse 11: For we who live are always delivered to death for Jesus sake, that the life of Jesus also may be manifested in our mortal flesh.

Verse 12: So then death is working in us, but life is in us

Verse 13: And since we have the same spirit of faith, according to what is written, "I believed and therefore I spoke, "we also believed and therefor speak.

Verse 14: Knowing that he who rose up the Lord Jesus will also raise us up with Jesus, and will present us with you.

Verse 15: For all things are for your sakes, that grace, having spread through the many, may cause thanksgiving to abound to the glory of God.

In this world times get hard. Being of the flesh, at times you'll feel defeated. Don't give up; because we have a treasure. His name is Jesus Christ and he lives in us. The treasures of Jesus shine through darkness. The treasure of Jesus shines through the difficult times.

Speaking of difficult times, I want to share a testimony that I heard a young lady share once. Being a single parent with two kids and had jut lost her job. She only had $187.13, which was the money for her light bill. Her refrigerator was base, and she didn't know whether to go and spend the light bill money on groceries or not. I also want to share that her lights were on the verge of being cut off. Putting so many applications in and not being called back after interviews, by not knowing which way to go as far as a decision, the young lady said that she felt perplexed and was in deep despair. She also shared that being a

Knowing Your Identity

child of God, she caused this crisis to allow her to forget her identity. Being of Christ, which was the treasure inside of her, the young lady said that, she went into her room and got down on her knees. As she closed her prayer out, the young lady said as she got up, she felt a sensation of victory. She went into the kitchen, made the kids a couple of ham and cheese sandwiches, afterwards they watched television and went to bed. That night as she slept, she felt that no matter what was going on, everything was going to be alright. The next morning when she work up, she gave the kids their last two bowls of cereal, and threw the box in the trash can. She didn't want to sacrifice dipping in the light bill money because, she was already behind, so the kids had no lunch money. The young lady shared of how she went to go in the refrigerator and get the last two slices of ham, and the last two slices of cheese. Once she retrieved it she got the last few slices of bread out of the bread box and one of the slices was the end piece. She said she heard a whisper saying. "Put the ham, cheese, and bread back. Give your kids their lunch money." Right then the young lady said she recognized the voice of the Lord because, it was a voice of reasons, and it soothed her soul. Immediately, she put the ham and cheese back in the refrigerator. The young lady also said that she put the four slices of bread back in the bread box. Then she went to her pocketbook and pulled out two five dollar bills. Be mindful lunch was only two dollars. So all she was supposed to give out to them was four dollars. By praying, and believing in God, she told them to get some ice cream too. After she took them to school. She was on her way home and her car's gas needle was on empty. The voice spoke to her again and said, "Fill this care up." After she filled up her car. She headed on home through the busy traffic. Once

Knowing Your Identity

she pulled in her yard, and got out of the car, she heard the phone ringing, as she made her way to the front door.

As she got in the house, she quickly ran to the phone, and to her surprise, it was the Manager of the accountant department from the Marriott hotel. He asked her was she still interested in the job that she applied for. After telling him yes and about to start the job the very next day, the young lady called the light bill company to see would they work with her until she gets paid. After the person on the phone at the light bill company put her information in the computer. They told her that it must be a mistake because her light bill wasn't due until next month. By being children of God and Jesus abiding in us as treasure we'll always hit the jackpot. Just like it says in verse 8-9. We are hard pressed on every side, yet not crushed; we are perplexed, but not in despair;

Verse 9: persecuted, but not forsaken; struck down but not destroyed:

It talks about the negative crisis that Satan brings in our lives that may cause us to want to give up. There's a positive side to it all and his name is Jesus. If you notice it speaks of what we are going through, then there is a comma. That comma stands for "but."

Here's a scenario of what we've just read. The young lady lost her job, but Jesus pulled her out. In these scriptures verses 8-9 the comma separates us from the negative side.

Jesus is always that treasure who puts the comma's in our lives. We've all had those times when it seemed like nothing was going to work out for us. The treasures of Jesus, which resides inside of us, turned it all around. In our

Knowing Your Identity

identity we must know of how it is of such great prestige to have the treasures of Jesus Christ in our live.

Knowing Your Identity

Chapter 25

Press On

Phillipians Chapter 3

Verses 12 – 16

In Chapter 2 – I elaborated on the fact that we are marked. Being children of god, Satan brings worldly pressures our way. No matter what. We must continue to press on. You may be a hard worker on the job and never get credit. It may seem as soon as you get paid, and pay your bills, you barely have the money to get the things that you would like to have. You'll say to yourself, "I'll get it the next time when I get paid." then something goes wrong with your car, and the things that you wanted to get are put off again. You may go to church, pray, and live according to the word of God faithfully but, for some reason it may seems that all of God's blessing are detouring you for some reason. In Children of God lives this happens. We must continue to keep the faith. We must continue to pray, and live according to the word of God. It's called pressing on. Together let's take a look at what Paul says about pressing on in Philippians Chapter 3 verses 12-16.

Verses 12: Not that I have already attained, or am already perfected: but I pressed on, that I may lay hold of that for which Christ Jesus has also laid hold of me.

Knowing Your Identity

Verse 13: Brethren, I do not count myself to have apprehends; but one thing I do, forgetting those things which are behind and reaching forward to those things which we are ahead,.

Verse 14: I press toward the goal for the prize of the upward call of God in Christ Jesus

Verse 15: Therefore let us, as many as are mature, have this mind; and if in anything you think otherwise, God will reveal even this to you.

Verse 16: Nevertheless, to the degree that we have already attained, let us walk by the same rule, let us be of the same mind.

On this spiritual walk it's going at tough. The storms are going to come. The read to heaven is not on easy road. The bible tells us so. Being of the flesh we are not, or will never be perfect. The only perfect person who's ever walked this earth was our Lord and Savior Jesus Christ. By Jesus residing inside of us we have the power to overcome anything that Satan brings our way. On this road that we are traveling to heaven, situations are going to arise, that will cause you to say, "I'm getting tired of traveling this read. I go to church. I pray, I live according the word of God, and nothing seems to be working out." That's actually what a lot of people who are children of God says when the going gets tough.

I want to cross reference and go to the back of Matthew Chapter 10 verse 34. Listen to what Jesus said. This will give us better insight about the road that we are traveling to heaven.

Knowing Your Identity

Verse 34: Do not think that I came to bring peace on earth. I did not come to bring peace but a sword. As you can see Jesus said that his word would basically stir up a lot of conflict.

The definition of the word conflict is: Prolonged fighting. 2. Disharmony between incompatible or antithetical persons, ideas, or interests. 3. Psychological. A struggle, often unconscious, between mutually exclusive impulse or desires. 4. To be in opposition; differ.

As far as trying to sabotage our identity as children of God, all four of these definitions of conflict are how Satan comes at us.

1. I shared about how hard we work on jobs and we seem to never have any money for ourselves because it all goes towards the bills, we find ourselves in a prolonged fight with the economy.

2. On this walk to heaven, people, who you loved or who you thought loved you, doesn't share the same interest as for a Christ, and you find yourself in a mental struggle, because they are doing everything that is not of God. You all don't share the same ideas or interest. Matter of fact nobody wants to be around you because they feel that your life is dull and boring.

3. This becomes a psychological struggle in your mind as for us dealing with your economic problems. People scuh as your girlfriend, boyfriend, husband, wife, and family, distance themselves away from you. This all becomes mental stress.

Knowing Your Identity

4. Then we become in the mode of opposition and began to differ with the thought of, "Is this walk with Jesus the right thing to do?" I'm here to tell you that it is. I'm also here to tell you to press on. This is the way that it's supposed to be. That shows that you are on the perfect walk with Jesus. Whatever we lose because of this road that we walk with Jesus to heaven, don't look back. Yu may say, "Ms. McRae it's easy to say but hard to do, "I'm here to make it easier for you. On this road to heaven Satan is going to come with his "A" game. His so called "A" game is dealing with the mind. Remember we elaborated on Job's situation. The devil took him through a lot but, he didn't give up. Job continued to press on through all that he went through. Whatever walked away or you lose on this road to heave. Jesus will bring it back, or restore it or them, in a more fashionable and better way. I'm not sharing what I heard. I'm sharing from experience. On this road to heaven I've had some pretty rough jobs in my life. But at the end I ended up retiring from Duke medical center. I had to press on though.

I want to cross reference again, and go to 2nd Corinthians Chapter 11 verses 22-23.

Verse 22: Are they Hebrews? So am I. Are they Israelites? So am I. Are they the seed of Abraham? So am I.

Verse 23: Are they ministers of Christ? I speak as a fool – I am more: in labors more abundant, in stripes above measure, in prisons more frequently, in deaths often.

Knowing Your Identity

Verse 24: From the Jews five times I received forty strips minus one.

Verse 25: Three times I was beaten with rods; once I was stoned; three times I was shipped wrecked; a night and a day I have been in the deep;

Verse 26: in journeys often, in perils of water, in perils of robes, in perils of my own countrymen, in perils of Gentiles, in perils in the city, in perils in the wilderness, in perils in the sea, in perils among false brethren;

Verse 27: in weariness and toils in sleeplessness of ten, in hunger in thirst, in fasting's often, in cold and nakedness

Verse 28: besides the other things, what comes up on me daily: my deep concern for all the churches.

Verse 29: who is weak, and I am not weak? Who is made to stumble, and I do not burn with indignation?

Verse 30: If I must boast, I will boast in the things which concern my infirmity

Verse 31: The God and Father of the Lord Jesus Christ, who is blessed forever, know that I am not lying.

Knowing Your Identity

Verse 32: In Damascus the governor, under Aretas the king was guarding the city of the Damascenes with a garrison, desiring to arrest me.

Verse 33: but I was let down in a basket through a window in the wall, and escaped from his hands.

This is what Paul shared with the Phillipians. We all know that before Paul converted his life to Christ he was a part of Satan clan. He seemed not to have a worry at all. As you can see after he was converted to Christ, and began to walk the road to heaven, problems bean to come his way. It's the way of the world and this is where satan roams. By us being children of God we will have those same experiences in different ways as we also travel the road to heaven.

I just want to say, on this road times may get hard, but we got to keep pressing on. Economic problems may try to overwhelm us but, we can't give up. Those people we love, may not want to be of Christ, and thing that we are living a dull and boring life, don't give up. Keep on walking with Jesus. In our mind; the devil may play mind games and may cause us to want to give up. Continue to press on. The road to heaven is not an easy road to travel. Only the strong survive. We got to keep moving. As far as the word of God, our mission is clear. We are on the road to heaven, and we can't allow nothing to stop us. Don't look back as far as

Knowing Your Identity

what was lost. We have the ultimate prize. That prize is Jesus. It is in our identity to press on with Jesus, no matter what's going on around us.

Knowing Your Identity

Chapter 26

It Ain't Over

John Chapter 11

Verses 1-44

By closing this book out, I want to back track and go to the gospel of John. I saved this for last because it's such power in these scriptures. In Chapter 11 verse 1-44, it talks about a man by the name of Lazarus. He was the brother of Mary and Martha.

These are the two women who showed Jesus great hospitality when he came to their home. While Martha cooked a nice meal for Jesus, Mary wiped his feet with her long beautiful black hair. She even used fragrant oil as well. We all know that at that day and time fragrant oil was a high commodity, and cooking food just to be cooking was a no-no. But when it came to Jesus their Lord and Savior, none of that mattered. It was all for the Love of Jesus.

When we go all out for Jesus. He'll go all out for us. As I shared Lazarus was sick, and by this sickness having him near dead, Jesus had left their house, and the town of Bethany. Mary and Martha sent word to him that their brother Lazarus was bad off sick, and didn't look as if he was going to make it. Hearing this horrible news because Jesus loved Martha, Mary, and Lazarus. He didn't hurry and come. In fact it states in verse 6, "he stayed gone two more days." Let's take a look at verses 1-6. This will give us insight when a situation seems so hopeless that Jesus does what he does for a reason.

Knowing Your Identity

Verse 1: Now a certain man was sick, Lazarus of Bethany, the town of Mary and her sister Martha.

Verse 2: It was that Mary who anointed the Lord with fragrant oil and wiped his feet with her hair, whose brother Lazarus was sick.

Verse 3: Therefore the sisters sent to him, saying "Lord behold, he whom you love is sick."

Verse 4: When Jesus heard that, he said, "This sickness is not unto death, but for the glory of God, that the son of God may be glorified through it.

Verse 5: Now Jesus loved Martha and her sister and Lazarus

Verse 6: So, when he heard that he was sick, He stayed two more days in the place where he was at.

Why do think Jesus did that? Being our Lord and Savior. He's supposed to hurry to a crisis. It says in verse 5 that" Jesus loved Marth, her and Lazarus. Why didn't he come right away then?

Because of this delay, this crisis causes Mary and Martha, to forget their identity. They began to panic and also fear. Inside of their bodies registered the fact that Jesus didn't care. I can hear Mary and Martha now." Jesus came to our house. Martha made him a very good meal. I washed his feet with fragrant oil, and I used my hair at that. Jesus even sat here and shared the word with us. Now that Lazarus is sick he doesn't want to come. So much for this great hospitality that we showed him." Being of the flesh this is how we react. Just

Knowing Your Identity

that quick due to a crisis Mary and Martha forgot about who Jesus was. To make this a lot more drastic Lazarus died. Jesus knew this because, he spoke of it, and he was all the way in another town.

From this point, we are going look at key verses. I do want you to go on and read verses 1-44 because it has a powerful message. Let's now look at verse 13. This will confirm now of how Jesus spoke of Lazarus death all the way in another town.

Verse 13: However, Jesus spoke of his death, but they thought that he was speaking about taking rest in sleep. Now that Lazarus was dead he was anxious to get back to Judea which was located the town of Bethany.

It took him four days to take this journey. As he walked, his disciples followed because, they knew that a miracle was about to be transpired. As he came into the town of Bethany people seen Jesus and also began to follow. Martha heard that Jesus was in town, so she let Mary at the house, and she went to meet him.

Seeing Jesus as the people followed him, Martha approached him still not realizing her identity she let Jesus have it. In verse 21 she said, "If you had been here, my brother would not have died."

Jesus looked at her and basically said, "Evidently, you didn't know who you and your sister was showing great hospitality too in your home. I'm the king of kings, The Lord of Lords, The Lion of Judah, The Prince of Peace, and you strength and song. I'm also called the Savior, and the Resurrection and the life.

Knowing Your Identity

Martha call your sister Mary and I need for you all too take me to the grave. There you'll see the powers that I possess. Let's take a look at verses 38-44.

Verse 38: Then Jesus, again groaning in Himself, came to the tomb. It was a cave, and a stone lay against it.

Verse 39: Jesus said, "Take away the stone." Martha, the sister of him who was dead, said to him, "Lord by this time there is a stench, for he has been dead for four days."

Verse 40: Jesus said to her, "Did I not say to you that if you would believer you would see the Glory of God."

Verse 41: Then they took away the stone from the place where the dead man was laying. And Jesus lifted up. His eyes and said, "Father, I thank you that you always hear me.

Verse 42: "And I know that you always hear me, but because of the people who are standing by I said this, that they may believe that you sent me."

Verse 43: Now when he said these things, He cried with a loud voice, "Lazarus, come faith!"

Verse 44: And he who had died come outbound hand and foot with grave clothes, and his face was wrapped with a cloth. Jesus said to them, "Loose him, and let him go."

Knowing Your Identity

As you can see Jesus raised the dead. From these scriptures, now you see, it can look hopeless, but when it comes to Jesus, it is not over until he says it's over. When it comes to our identity, we'll panic when it all seems hopeless. But, when we have Jesus in our lives we can always count on him to raise us up above it all. In our identity we must always know that no matter how hard times of or situations get. It's is not over until God say it's over. What a mighty God that we serve.

Knowing Your Identity

Author's Notes

I really hope, and pray, that you've enjoyed the spiritual blessing from this book!!! It's so very important that the message of God is spreaded throughout the world!!! In fact God's word is our blueprint to life. In order for us, as children of God, to maintain our identity, the word has to be applied on an all-day basis. Due to Satan's craftiness, living in this world, can be as if we're living in a boxing ring. Satan throws blows at us because of our identity. The word of God teaches us to bob, weave, and duck those blows. Satan is constantly swinging at us. Forty great men who were inspired by God wrote the sixty-six books in the bible. If you read the bible, and relate it to the world, you'll see that everything that the bible speaks of has come into existence. The point that I'm getting at is, "Are You Ready?" Its harvest time and Jesus is coming!!! If you're ready. I ask that you accept Jesus Christ as your personal Lord and Savior!!! God instilled in my heart to write and tell you this!!! I can see how those 40 great men, who wrote the bible, were indeed inspired by God. God also inspired me. Honestly...I couldn't rest until I did it. In this message, I illustrated the bible to everyday experiences. I felt that by us dealing with sickness, financial burdens, relationships, job issues, etc., this book will give us the impulse, to recognize the enemy, and his tactics. So please, shine up your gold if it's tarnished, and say this sinner's prayer of redemption with me.

Father God. I come to you as a sinner. And want to receive the Lord Jesus Christ in my life. For I know with my heart, that he died and rose from the grave. Father God and I believe this with all of my heart. I thank you God for sacrificing your son for me. I know that Jesus died on the cross at Calvary for my sins and

Knowing Your Identity

transgressions. I do believe in the blood. UI ask Jesus to come into my life. Cleanse me from the worldly issues that I've been a part of. Lord…and I thank you for saving me.

If you said that prayer welcome back in the pastures of God. Just like that, you've recognized your identity. Together we're walking in the rays of heaven!!! It's been such a joy to share the word of God with you!!!!

Doris V. McRae

It was an honor to publish my grandmother's book. My wife Carolyn, and I worked so very hard to help my grandmother share the word of God, with the audience, and the whole world. Never…do or will we ever forget where our help comes from.

Father God we thank you for doing everything that we can't do for ourselves. We…owe it all to you. Almighty God we thank. If we had ten thousand tongues, we couldn't praise you enough!!!

Country &Carolyn Getter-McRae

Knowing Your Identity

May God Bless you!

Made in the USA
Middletown, DE
02 May 2024